A Death

in the Family

Books by Paul Carroll

The Black Pages
A Death in the Family
The Undying and the Dead
Second Sight of Sort Eyes

The Rebirth Cycle
Balor Reborn
The Hounds of Hell
The Blood of Leap
Old Gods & Wicked Things

Standalone Titles
Tales of the Fantastical (Vol. 1)
Stepping Forward

Anthologies
Dublin's Fierce City
Fierce Mighty
Fierce New World
Fierce & Proud
Fiercepunk

paulcarrollwriter.com

The Black Pages

The Reaper · Book 1

A Death
in the Family

Paul Carroll

First published by Paul Carroll at paulcarrollwriter.com

ISBN: 9798694527507

For my friends, who encourage me to bring my work to life.

Table of Contents

𝒫ROLOGUE

There is an old saying that violence often begets further violence. On New Year's Eve, 2016, that statement could not have been closer to the truth. Premature fireworks exploded over New York, a few eager celebrators lighting up early. The cheers of the countdown began. What had been a hellish year for almost all involved was soon coming to an end.

Ten.

Unfortunately for some, the night was not made up of festivities. In particular, Carlson Grimes was having a tough time as midnight approached, with an especially fatal stab wound in his stomach attempting to beat the matching wounds around his body for blood loss. He had propped himself up against the wall in an alley, no more phone, no more wallet, and the effects of his last few drinks quickly fading as he failed to hold himself together.

It was not how he had meant the night to go. It was not how *he* had intended to go, either. He had wanted to bow out in a blaze of glory. Or, maybe, pissing himself at an old folks' home. He hadn't really decided which one sounded better. But neither of them involved a lonely, painful death by multiple knife wounds.

Nine.

Carlson wasn't sure if the blood loss was messing with his mind, but he could have sworn that something was wrong with the world as he sat there waiting for death. Time was slower. He could feel it like water washing over his skin

— or, more relevant to his current predicament, blood gushing down to his belt.

"So, this is it…" he mumbled.

"I'm afraid so," a voice responded. Carlson looked up at him – judging by the voice that it was, in fact, a man - and his heart skipped a beat. "Yes, I know. My appearance is somewhat…unsettling."

The man stood just shy of seven-feet, though his feet appeared to have been tucked up underneath the great, black robe that fell in waves of smoke and shadow to the ground. His clothes were tattered and torn, spilling out darkness with every passing moment that Carlson stared at him, so that he began to block out everything around him. The alley was vanishing.

As unnerving as the robe was, the man's face was at least doubly so. Where there ought to have been flesh, skin, a discomforting smile, was the toothy grin of a naked skull. It almost glimmered white, spotless and clean as if the man brushed it twice daily with a toothbrush. His lower jaw clung to the rest of his head without the need for muscle or cartilage. It did not move as he spoke. The words had merely *come* from him. If he breathed, it was through the holes in his face where the nose ought to have been.

He had no eyes, which made Carlson's skin crawl. Instead, there were floating, glowing orbs of violet light. They stared with the ferocity of a lion on the prowl, and poured out a coldness the likes of which men only spoke of in myths.

As if he needed further confirmation of the man's identity, Carlson needed only to follow a long, bony arm to a skeletal hand clutching what could best be assumed to be a Scythe. It seemed impossibly long, taller than the man by a couple of feet, with a blade at least twice as long as a man was wide. Along its bottom, the blade shone with a violet light, identical in tone and severity to the man's eyes.

"Are you… him?" Carlson asked.

The expressionless face emanated despondence. Motionlessly, he said, "Death, you mean? Yes. If you like."

Eight.

"And this is real? You're really here? For me?"

Death sighed, and a streetlight exploded. "Would you believe that you aren't the first person to ask so many questions?" He tapped the handle of the Scythe against the ground, and the glass from the light rushed back into place as if nothing had happened. "Yes, Carlson Grimes, I am here for you. I have been waiting all night for you to die. You are my last job of the year, and it has been a very, very long year."

The darkness from Death's robe poured out further in every direction. The streetlight blipped from sight. There was only Carlson, Death, the bloodied floor of the alley, and the brick wall against which Carlson was dying. The reality of the situation was beginning to cement itself in his mind.

"Now, if you have no further questions, I'd like to get started."

Carlson raised a hand. Death almost sighed again. The world seemed to shiver as he held it back. "I do have questions," he told his skeletal companion. "Like, why didn't you do anything to stop this?"

"There are certain things in life that are unavoidable, and certain rules that must be obeyed. There is a protocol. There are procedures. There is a hierarchy of supernatural needs that need to be met, an order to things." His words pounded in Carlson's ears. He almost worried that Death would deafen him. "If you were due to fall in love in February, but due to die in December, your death takes precedence. This is the way of the world. If you wanted more time, if I had interfered with the way of mortal doings, you would have met your end some other way."

"If you had not been stabbed eleven times tonight, if I had stepped in before that man could have done anything to you, you would have caused more pain and sorrow to the world than you could possibly imagine. You would not have a choice in the matter. There are demands to be met."

Carlson couldn't help himself when he shouted, "You mean you were just standing there, watching it happen?" Death shrugged. "I didn't see you there. And you're not hard to miss."

"I will take that as your final question," came the booming response. "Mortal eyes cannot perceive much of this world. People like me go by unnoticed every day. It is the way of things." He lowered the blade of the Scythe towards Carlson. He wasn't sure if its light made him feel as cold as he did, or if it was the blood loss.

Seven.

The word echoed from a distance. They were getting close to midnight. More importantly, they were reaching the end of a year that had been dreadful, on so many levels that Carlson could barely keep up. Politically, a nightmare. Culturally, a disaster. Personally, hell. Professionally, worse. And yet…

"I don't want to die."

The words escaped Carlson's mouth before he had time to think about them. They came straight from his soul, which he felt for the first time in his life inside his body, screaming at the presence of the Scythe that called for it like a greedy child.

"You must," Death responded. "The Scythe will pull your soul from your body, that you might move on more easily to the great Beyond, and your body will be free to die without risk of keeping you here. It is the way things have to be, particularly given your unwillingness to let go of the past. Words have proven to never be enough for you."

"What do you know?" Carlson spat.

The skeletal face seemed to loom closer. "More than you would like me to."

Six.

The Scythe came closer still to Carlson's chest. His heart pounded furiously. Blood was pouring from his wounds more quickly. His stomach had gotten numb to the pain. His head was getting light.

He knew that he couldn't survive this. Not without help. Not without blood. Not that Death cared. He stared at the glowing eyes with so much hate, he could barely contain himself. This was not how he imagined the year ending. Even in his wildest dreams, even with the world becoming stranger by the minute, he couldn't have imagined *this.*

He didn't know what he was doing when he grabbed the Scythe by the handle. Death seemed caught off guard by this sudden movement. Carlson tugged at it, doing his best to keep the blade from pressing against him, while struggling to get the handle out of Death's grip. Even with his injuries, Carlson was winning the fight.

"Wait, you can't do this," Death told him.

"Watch me," Carlson retorted, and jerked it loose from the skeletal man that stood over him.

Five.

Anyone who has ever been granted power beyond mortal understanding knows exactly how Carlson felt when he held the Scythe in his hands for the first time. For everyone else, imagine a storm brewing inside your very heart, shooting bolts of lightning through every nerve in your body, wrapping around bones like a million terrifying snakes, pouring into your muscles, filling every bit of you until you felt ready to burst. Then, multiply it by a factor of ten.

Carlson's body was not capable of managing such an experience, and his injuries had little to do with it. He didn't know it, but without the proper permission, the Scythe was a dangerous thing for a mortal man to hold. But he did know this: as much as the Scythe wanted to get away from Carlson Grimes's grip, it was nothing compared to the man's desire to live

The storm in his body was winning the battle, and so were the open wounds. But with the Scythe in his hand, Carlson came to understand that the body need only be a temporary thing. With a scream that seemed to fragment the very essence of reality, his very soul tore loose from his body, a glowing, violet likeness of the man he thought himself to be.

Four.

He stared at Death with renewed hatred. The robed figure seemed to shrink back from him, and his darkness fell back within his clothing. The world was opening itself up to Carlson, freshly armed and utterly disembodied. He took ghostly steps towards Death, laughing to himself as his body bled out.

"It's screaming in my hands, you know," he told Death. "It wants to get back to you, but it knows that it can't. And so do you. You're powerless without your Scythe. You're just a man in a cloak, and if you ever think about taking it off… Well, who knows what will happen to you?"

The skeletal man shook his head in disbelief. "This can't be happening." He looked down at his hands. There was nothing of him there, and his face was the same. Just a skeleton under a hood.

"Take off the robe, and everyone will see you," Carlson told him. "But without this," he said, holding up the Scythe, "You'll be trapped in this fancy little time-deprived existence of yours. Dangerous for a mortal man, but fine for someone who can't be seen or touched, right?"

Three.

"It's almost midnight. If you're lucky, you might get a good view of the fireworks." Carlson turned his back on

Death, walking towards the main road. "Attempt to follow me, and I'll make you regret it," he added.

New York was buzzing with life. In his new state of being, Carlson could see it all, the electricity in the air, the explosion of celebration, the anticipation of possibility and the chance of something new as the worst year in recent memory came to an end. The universe had seemed to fall apart on them, between celebrity deaths and nasty politics, but now he could understand why people partied at midnight. Now he could understand what it was that people were doing when they came together, to count down to the end of the year with their loved ones.

He was his own source of light in the world, and he held the most powerful tool any dead man could hope to acquire. The Scythe did not want him near it, but he held on tightly nonetheless. It groaned at the strain of keeping him out of its inner workings. He could feel its impossible consciousness fighting him, trying not to give him any information that he might find useful.

But it wasn't ready for this. Death had not been ready for this. Carlson hadn't been ready, either, but 2016 had been a year of surprises to him.

Two.

He felt the knowledge flood into his body, unsorted and almost useless. Protocol. Procedure. Everything Death had told him before.

And then, in the midst of everything he didn't care to know, he found a way to use the Scythe, a way of making the most of a deadly situation. He let out a voracious laugh, dancing in the middle of the road to the sound of windows smashing all around him. Car alarms sang for him. People cried out in shock, in disgust, in annoyance. None of them could hear Carlson Grimes as he moved swiftly through the city, streets pouring around him as he zipped from his body's location to the far side of the city in, what felt to him at least, a matter of seconds.

He scoured the neighbourhood around him, eyes peeled for life.

Music reached his ears from an apartment overhead. He didn't know this part of town. He didn't know these people. With a blink of a ghostly eye, he was in the room with them, a bunch of fresh-out-of-college jocks counting down to midnight with their high-school-sweethearts. A television in the corner had the countdown on display.

One.

He looked them all over. Many of them were overweight, fat from years of partying and drinking and gaining weight to hold a position on the pitch. One looked like he'd given up the sport completely, thin and weak compared to his friends. His eyes landed on a man with wisdom in his eyes, a trim waist, and a beautiful girl in his arm.

Carlson could smell their souls over the stench of beer and fried food. He could feel their pulses, pushing out into the world as they celebrated the end of the year. Their souls were glowing bright and fresh.

He weaved through the room towards his mark, completely invisible to the crowd. He could see the strength in the man's body, the gears whirring in his brain, the lust for life in his heart. He gripped the Scythe tightly, and placed a glowing hand on the man's chest.

"Happy New Year," the room cheered.

Carlson cheered with them, clinking a glass of rum and coke against vodka and beer. He kissed the girl in his arm, tasting her drink on her lips, feeling stronger than he'd ever been in his life.

And he was only getting started.

CHAPTER ONE: NEW YEAR...

Bang. Bang. Bang.

The sound echoed in Benjamin Cooper's head as if the knocking was against his skull. His eyes peeled open a fraction, and closed immediately. Ben didn't know what time it was, except to say that it was, by all accounts, too early. Too early to open his eyes. Too early to be awake. Much too early for someone to be knocking on the front door.

He did the math: Four cans of beer. Three vodka-jello shots. Six rum and cokes. And three more loud knocks on the front door.

Bang. Bang. Bang.

He tried to add it all up in his head. He totalled too much alcohol, one bad hangover, and sixteen swear words from his mother as she stomped through the house. The knocks continued, in sets of three.

Bang. Bang. Bang.

He rolled over in bed, wrapped his pillow around his head to block out as much sound as possible. He could still hear the banging from downstairs pounding in his head, and a whisper in his ear to move, to answer, to do anything.

"Everyone up," his mother called from the front door. He barely heard her. Her voice was strained and tired. His head was full of the sound of the banging at the front door, and his stomach too full of last night's mistakes to care enough. The Coopers didn't do New Year's half-assed, and were paying the price for it now. Eventually, he rolled out of bed, landing painfully on the floor. He could have stayed there for another few hours, if he'd been allowed.

His door opened quickly. "Come on," his sister, Jean, said to him. Their Golden Labrador bounded into the room, licking at Ben's face, prodding at him with her paw. "Macy, that means you too," Jean scolded.

Jean was a couple of years younger than Ben, but he always imagined that she had her life a little more together than he had so far managed. He had studied Art History in college, leaving him so-far underemployed. Jean had chosen to study Business, with a minor in Computer Science. She was barely out of her graduation gown when she'd begun working properly. Neither one of them could afford the luxury of freedom from the family home. So she said, anyway.

He climbed awkwardly to his feet, the room spinning around him as Jean and Macy left him to compose himself. The house was cold. It was almost always cold in the winter. No one seemed to mind. Ben wondered if, maybe, it was because no one wanted to pay the heating bill.

"Ben, where are you?" his father shouted up the stairs. Twenty-four didn't seem to be an appropriate age to stop treating his son like a teenager. Years away from the family home, though, had almost given Ben enough of a backbone to pretend his father didn't think he was a hopeless good-for-nothing. Almost.

There were certain things that the Coopers did well. They were excellent drinkers. They were studious, occasionally well-mannered, generally likeable, and always paid their debts.

Other things, they were not so good with. The morning-after, for one. Asserting themselves towards greater ambitions, for another. Only Jean had really escaped that family curse. And, the thing Ben considered the family's biggest flaw, they were less than experts when it came to inter-family communications.

Ben didn't mind the shouting. He didn't mind the swearing. He didn't mind that his parents had routines and often forgot that he and Jean had their own schedules to manage. What bothered him – what had always bothered him – was that the Cooper family seemed intent on keeping a great number of things a secret from one another. He had kept his eating disorder a secret when he was in college, until Jean called him out on it over Christmas dinner during his final year. She had managed to hide depression and anxiety from their parents, but in true style broke the cycle of secrecy enough to talk to Ben long into the night whenever she really needed to.

Always, he had developed his doubts about his parents, who never seemed to have any secrets from their children. This wouldn't have been a problem for most people, Ben knew, except that he knew that the Coopers were notorious for keeping things from each other for as long as possible. Secrets, he knew, always came out.

When he could finally see the front door, still wide-open despite the cold January chill pouring violently into their house, he wished that he had been wrong about his parents. He had never wished for a more honest family more than when he laid his eyes upon their loud and uninvited guest for the first time.

Dressed all in black, with a face of bone and a glowing-red Scythe in his hand, was Death. It was not the most ideal start to the year that the Coopers could have imagined.

Amanda Cooper, Ben's mother, chef and cleaner, ordered them all into the living room. She swept crumbs from an armchair for their guest, who smiled at her with a face full of teeth, and not much else. He sat down gratefully in the armchair, as if he weighed nothing at all, and crossed his hands on his lap. His Scythe was nowhere to be seen.

The rest of the Coopers were sat around the coffee table on couches to either side of their guest. Ben sat beside Jean, opposite their parents. Macy plonked herself at his feet, keeping them warm in lieu of slippers. The coffee table was littered with beer cans and discarded plastic shot glasses, stained with spilled liquor and paved in crumbs. Ben's father, Martin, had cleared just enough room for five cups of tea. Amanda had forgotten to ask what her guest liked to drink, or how he took it.

They sat in silence.

Ben counted plastic glasses. Martin held his wife's hand tightly. Amanda bit her lip. Macy yawned. And Jean had had enough. It took only thirty seconds for her to open her mouth. "Who are you here for, Mister…"

Death looked at her blankly. "You can call me Gary."

"Gary?" she repeated. He nodded slowly. "You're the Grim Reaper, and you're telling us that your name is Gary?"

Ben had never seen a skeleton sigh. He had never seen one in real life, of course, but they often came without the benefit of lungs. Or consciousness. So, when Gary sighed, Ben shivered. Part of it was because the man's mouth never once moved. Part of it was that Gary's breath, which poured out of him from every orifice in his long, black robe, was icy cold. And, most concerning to Ben, when Gary sighed, the sound spilled right into Ben's ears as if he were merely imagining the sound.

"Perhaps I shouldn't have come in uniform," the skeleton said to himself. The words bounced around in Ben's head. He could see from the look on his father's face that he wasn't the only one feeling it. Gary turned his head towards Amanda. "May I use your restroom? Preferably one where someone hasn't thrown up."

Lip quivering, Amanda told him, "Up the stairs, first door you'll see."

He bounded up the stairs swiftly and quietly. Ben listened for his steps, but there were none. Gary seemed to float along the ground by the torn-up tails of his robe, along a path of black vapour. When he moved up the stairs, he appeared to be walking, but the squeaky steps remained silent. Only the door to the bathroom made any noise, closing gently behind the spectral man.

The Coopers stayed still, listening out for any further sounds from upstairs. Macy had her ears trained, but eventually she resigned herself to a further yawn, and planted herself back down on Ben's feet.

"Can someone tell me what's going on?" Jean asked.

"I think he needed to use the toilet," Ben told her. He tried not to picture the Grim Reaper standing in his bathroom. His sister glared at him. "Or, maybe not."

"I was afraid this day would come," Amanda said quietly.

Martin hushed her, which only served to draw further attention from their children. The elder Coopers exchanged worried looks. It was the sort of look one gave when they had news, but when they couldn't quite tell if it was going to be taken as good news or bad news. Ambiguous news. Questionable news.

A secret.

"There's a lot to explain," Martin said to his children.

"Then start at the beginning," Jean responded. Ben was glad not to be the one she was annoyed at. "Start with why you would ever expect Death himself to show up on our front door. Or, you know, how you even knew there was a *literal* Death."

Amanda hesitated. Martin stammered over his words. And the bathroom door opened upstairs.

The steady rhythm of footsteps on the stairs turned every head in the room. The right steps squeaked under plain loafers. An average, fleshy hand held the bannister. A warm smile greeted the Coopers. Gary, in the flesh, looked to be nearing forty. His hair was a curly mess, his eyes looked tired, and he was a little on the pale side.

He was, undoubtedly, human.

"You all look like you've seen a ghost," he said to them, taking his place in the armchair again. The cushion sank under his weight. His sweater bunched up against him. Mismatched socks popped out from under his trousers. Ben noticed a wedding ring on his ring.

"You're Death?" Ben asked him. "You're the tall dude with the sickle and the robes and a face from a cold case post-mortem?"

Gary shrugged. "The uniform is just part of the job. And it's a Scythe, not a sickle. We're very particular about the naming." The Coopers stared at him silently. "Look, I know this isn't the best timing. I know it's early, and I know last night wasn't exactly a quiet night for anyone, but that's why I'm here. It's a new year. It's a new opportunity for people like me, and people like... well, you."

He spoke to the family, avoiding direct eye contact with any of the human members of the family. Macy looked at him fondly, but stayed put on Ben's feet. Gary sat still, hands crossed.

Ben raised a hand. "Which one of us is going to die?" Jean slapped his knee. "I mean it," he said to her. "That's what you're here for, right? That's what Death shows up for. Someone's going to die."

"Ben," Amanda said flatly.

"No, I want to know. Is it me?"

Gary raised a hand, and the Coopers ceased any attempt to start an argument. "Usually, you would be right. I'd show up, collect a soul, and be on my merry, skeletal way to the next on the list. It's a busy job. It's necessary, but it's tiring. And while I would normally be here to take a soul because someone's being held back from moving on, that's not why I'm here today."

He sighed, and Ben realised that whenever Gary spoke, it was as if he were just another human. He commanded the room, but he was otherwise no different to the Coopers. That thought brought less peace to him than he would have liked.

"There's a lot you might not realise about the world," Gary said to them. "There's magic around every corner. There's a whole phone book filled with supernatural businesses and freelance mystics, if you know where to find it. And there are people like me, who work behind the scenes, more hidden from the world than the magicians and the witch doctors. Reapers."

The room began spinning again. Ben grabbed the arm of the couch, and rushed to his feet as quickly as he could. Macy jumped out of his way instinctively, watching him fall into the downstairs restroom.

His stomach emptied in one quick lurch.

After cleaning himself up, Ben stumbled back into the living room. "Sorry," he muttered. Macy took up her place at his feet when he sat down again.

"Like I said, last night wasn't quiet," Gary said with a chuckle.

Jean stared at him. "You keep saying 'job'. Why?" Ben noted that she had avoided the longer conversation about magic and the supernatural. She went straight to the point of getting this stranger out of their house.

Gary fiddled with his wedding ring. "Everyone does something," he said plainly. "You're a busy woman, in an uncompromising field. Your mother is a florist. Your father is an accountant. Your brother is... maybe underutilised on a professional level. And I'm a Reaper. It pays the bills. It puts food on my family's table. And contrary to popular belief, I don't hurt anybody by doing what I do." He smiled at her in a failed attempt at making light of the subject. "But I'm done," he told her.

Amanda whimpered audibly, and Martin hushed her. It didn't help with Jean's suspicions.

"How can you be done?" Ben asked him. He decided to give Gary's swipe at him the benefit of the doubt, if only because he was afraid of what would happen if the Reaper took out his Scythe again.

"It's a job, like any other," Gary explained. "And last night, I quit. It was too tough a year. Too many people of high renown dying. Too much despair. Too much to fight against, between my feelings and those of other people. I've been in the job for fifteen years. That's longer than most, and I'm hanging up the Scythe, so to speak."

Martin cleared his throat. "They don't know about this sort of stuff," he said to Gary. "They don't know about you and the others." He looked to his children, while Amanda fought back tears. "We didn't, either. Not for a long time," he told them. "It sort of just shows up whenever you most need it."

Jean remained silent. Ben hadn't seen her like that before. She asked the questions he was afraid to, and always had.

Gary just nodded. "It's before my time, but the Scythe keeps records. Twenty-five years ago, give or take, a deal was made." He looked to Ben and Jean specifically. "Your parents took out the supernatural equivalent of a mortgage. They needed something the natural world couldn't provide them, something money couldn't buy. There was a price, and now, with my imminent retirement, it's collection time."

"We always thought we would have more time before this happened," Amanda whispered. Everyone heard her over the silence. "We never knew when to expect any of this. What to expect at all, really. We just…"

Martin hugged her tightly when she started to cry. Gary shifted uncomfortably in his seat.

"The size of your deal, it was quite a big ask I'm told," Gary continued, this time addressing the Cooper parents. He tried not to look at them as he spoke. "There are usually only a few ways to pay it off. You were made aware of some of them back then, I'm sure, but it's typically a 'loaner's discretion' sort of arrangement."

Martin stood up. It was unexpected and sudden. Macy didn't know what to make of it. Gary tried his best not to react. It was obvious to Ben and Jean that the Reaper preferred to wear his uniform for his job, to hide his face from those he was talking to. He wasn't, it seemed, very good at masking his expressions.

"All my affairs are in order," Martin announced. "You can take my life as payment. We knew it might come to this."

"What, dad?" Jean gasped.

Amanda pulled a cushion to her face to cry into. Ben started putting everything together in his head. Why his parents were so conservative with their spending. Why his father, a mere fifty-five years old, had drawn up his final will and testament so many years ago. Why his mother kept on working, even when it seemed like they didn't necessarily need the money. They were waiting for this day, for the day when Martin Cooper, husband, father, dog-owner, would willingly give up his life for his family.

Ben didn't have a chance to vocalise his opinion on any of this, when Gary waved a hand casually. "I'm not here for you, Mister Cooper. Please sit down." Martin remained standing, back straight, chest out, belly barely contained by his t-shirt. "*Sit*," Gary repeated, and the force of the word carried through the air. Martin collapsed into his chair beside Amanda. "I'm here for Ben," Gary said quietly.

Gaelic folklore spoke of the banshee, the wailing woman. Her voice would cry out loudly when someone was going to die. It would rattle bones. It would break glass. It would chill the very soul. The noise that came out of Amanda Cooper's mouth put the banshee's cries to shame.

Mothers never wished to outlive their children.

While Amanda screamed, and Ben worried that she might hurt herself in her outburst of grief, Jean and Martin looked to him sadly. He was still catching up to the words.

Gary placed a hand on Amanda's shoulder. "You needn't cry," he told her. "Like I said before, loaner's discretion." He smiled at Amanda when she looked up at him, blinded by her own tears, face red and puffy. "They don't want his soul. They don't want him to die. They want him to become Death."

There were a number of perks of the job for those who took up the mantle of Death. A full Health and Dental plan in place, with specific emphasis on the pearly whites, for dramatic effect. The hours were flexible, enough that a Reaper could still live a regular life. The pay was more than decent; considering his choice in college major, Ben hadn't ever thought he'd be earning as much as Gary offered him. There were also, Gary told him, plenty of opportunities to travel. It was, he said, a requirement of the job.

"What about the downsides?" Jean asked. "No job is that good."

"Aside from the obvious nature of the job that would leave you watching a lot of people dying, there are sometimes some minor global disturbances that need to be seen to that could exhaust you. Just slightly." Gary tried to smile. He wasn't doing a great job of it. "Grief does funny things to the world. We have enough people on staff to clean up afterwards, but it's up to people like me to put an end to the weirdness."

"You saw yourself when you showed up, right?" Ben asked. "Put an end to the weirdness? All of this is weird. And you just expect us to accept it. What, I'm supposed to just take over for you? What if I don't want to? What if I had other plans for my life?"

Jean took Ben's hand in hers, while Macy pawed at his leg. Amanda and Martin looked up from the couch. She still looked shaken, but she had at least stopped crying.

Gary waved his hand, and the Scythe popped into view in a splash of red light. The Reaper held it in his hand, his eyes glowing to the hue of the blade. "Your father dies if you don't accept the job. That's the only other price they'll accept." Ben looked down to his parents. They avoided eye contact. Jean gave his hand a squeeze. He knew she didn't want to state the obvious to him. "It's not permanent," Gary added, "Just a few years. They'll iron out the details after a couple of weeks."

Ben nodded. "Just… put the Scythe away. I'll do it."

Jean pulled him into a hug. They hadn't hugged like that in longer than he could remember. When had they stopped being close in that way, he wondered? When had they stopped being the children who grew up doing everything together?

"I can't put the Scythe away, Ben. It's yours now. Effective immediately, you're taking over my role as Reaper. You know what they say, New Year, New You."

Paul Carroll

Chapter Two: The Underwood Case

Ben was afforded the luxury of a hot shower, a change of clothes, and breakfast, before Gary would take him out on his first assignment. He settled for two out of three, when his stomach couldn't quite settle at the thought of food. He scrubbed away the night before, last year's Ben, and threw on whatever clothes he could find that were both handy and clean.

Leaving the Cooper house led them to a neighbourhood that Ben wasn't familiar with. A simple step through the doorway, and poof – they stood outside a small, quaint house in desperate need of a paint job, its garden long overgrown, and the front gate hanging off its hinges. "We're not in Kansas anymore," Ben remarked.

"Arkansas, actually, so close," Gary told him.

Ben tried to wrap his head around the journey. "We were just in New York. You understand that, right? How did we get here?" Gary took Ben's arm in his right hand, and clicked the fingers of his left. The Scythe popped into place in Ben's hand, glowing red along the base of the blade. "This thing?"

"Everything you do during your time as a Reaper will be through the Scythe. It'll guide the souls, and it'll guide you. Cops have partners, you have this." Gary looked at the blade longingly. "It's the closest thing you'll have to a friend while you're on the job. Don't forget that, Ben."

The Scythe seemed to sing in Ben's head, a song composed of the glistening of metal, a choir of death blaring wordless chants into his ears. It felt like a greeting, and a warning. There was so much to this that Ben was struggling to wrap his head around.

"There's a protocol to the job," Gary explained. "It's straightforward, really. Head inside with the Scythe out, uniform on if you prefer. We'll leave that for another day, when you'll be in a more crowded environment."

Ben's hand instinctively touched his face. He imagined himself without his skin. He would lose himself to the skull, he thought. There would be nothing left of him. "Does it hurt? Wearing the uniform, I mean. Losing your skin like that."

Gary smiled back at him. "It's painless, but I understand the apprehension. I was your age when I took on the job. You finally think you're comfortable in your own flesh, and then you have to take it all away for your job. Corporate life is like that. You compromise the things you hold dear for the sake of something that seems to be bigger than you. But it doesn't hurt. It's mostly an illusion, and it's entirely for the benefit of the people we visit. The uniform has its own magic." Ben nodded. He wasn't sure he understood, but Gary looked like he was trying, so that would be good enough for him, for now. "Step two, when you enter the scene: find the person who's going to die."

Ben's first thought was that it shouldn't be difficult to find someone in their own home. Then, he thought about everything he saw in the news. Terrorist attacks. Wars. Gas leaks. Mass shootings. How do you find the one person whose soul you're supposed to take if there are dozens of people dying all around you?

The Scythe sang in his head. He didn't understand it as words, but he thought he knew what it meant. He tried not to think about how it knew to respond to anything.

"Step three," Gary continued, "is to convince the person to pass quietly."

His mother's cries rang through Ben's ears. There was no quiet in death. There was always going to be pain. "What if they don't want to die?"

"Very few people truly wish to die," Gary told him. "But you need to let them know how painless it'll be. You need to let them see the reality of their situation for themselves. The Scythe can help, but this is why there are mortal Reapers behind the blade. We understand death, you and I, more than the Scythe ever can. If you can figure out how to communicate it to someone, you make your job easier, and their pain lesser."

Gary, in all his experience, made it seem like a walk in the park. Go to a house. Talk to someone. Simple. Ben knew he was missing something, some key detail in all of this. "What's the Scythe for, then?"

The blade sang with delight in his ears.

"When you've convinced someone to pass, place the blade against their chest. Their soul will be ripped from their bodies and pulled into the Scythe. It's an extradimensional tool, many thousands of years older than we can work out. It knows what to do. That's step four. Step five, will the soul to HQ. The Scythe will respond accordingly."

The walk in the park suddenly felt like it was during a storm. And the park was on fire.

"You can do this, Ben," Gary told him. "Your first case should be easy." He pulled a file out of thin air. Ben wondered if he'd ever figure that out, or if he'd need to carry a dozen different folders with him every day just to get by for however long he was supposed to be taking lives. "Her name is Martha Underwood. She's a widow. Long-term cancer sufferer. Grandkids are all grown up, and all over the country. She's alone. And she's finally going to die." He sighed, and added, "Eventually, all of this will seem like just part of the job. You won't feel so bad for everyone."

Ben wasn't sure if that was supposed to make him feel better, or if he was supposed to just roll with it. Maybe there was a reason Gary was leaving, after all this time. He'd been a Reaper for longer than Ben had been eligible to work, even part-time. He'd been at it for nearly half his life. And here he was, ready to give it up. Ben saw the way he watched the Scythe. It was like if Ben had to give away Macy. Or if he had to give up ever spending time with Jean again.

He wondered when he would stop feeling so bad for Gary, and the Scythe sang him a soft tune in his head.

Step one: enter the house. The door opened itself to Ben. Or, he presumed, to the Scythe. He heard it sing a song in his mind just as the lock undid itself. A gentle breeze blew from behind him, pushing the door inwards. A beam of light split the house down the middle. Martha Underwood's house was dark, cluttered, and messy. Ben wondered at what point she had stopped caring about cleaning it up. He imagined it might have been the last time she had had a visitor.

Well, now she had one. A visitor. Her last visitor.

Ben eased through the mess of unopened mail on the floor. Late payments of bills. Overdue mortgage payments. A black-lined envelope mixed in among the stamped-red final-warnings. He wanted to pick it all up for her, but he knew it wouldn't make a difference now. Not with his arrival. Not with Gary on his heels.

Step two: find the person who's due to die. It felt like it should have been easier, but from the look of things, Martha had made a hiding place for herself in every corner of the house. Stacks of old magazines stood high on the coffee table. The curtains were drawn tightly shut, sealing out the world. Unfolded laundry was piled up on a dingy ironing board. A cupboard under the stairs was open and overflowing.

The stench of rotting food poured from the kitchen, blending with stale breath and fevered sweat. It filled every dark corner in the old house.

Martha's whole life was falling down within this one room. It took Ben a few minutes to progress beyond the doorway. He finally found her in the kitchen, sitting with a dirty glass of yellowed water. Her eyes were shut, her breaths came slowly and strained against her throat, and her lips were blackened.

She didn't acknowledge his entrance.

Step three: talk to her. Attempt to convince her to pass quietly. "Miss Underwood, can you hear me?" She remained almost perfectly still, save for a flicker of her eyes. "My name is…" He turned to Gary. "Do I tell her my name?"

The older man nodded. "When you're not in uniform, the human approach works best, and humans have names."

"I'm Benjamin Cooper. People call me Ben. Your front door was open."

She shook her head. "Lie," she said simply. Her voice was rough and untrained. She sounded as bad as her house looked. Martha's eyes opened slowly. "The door was locked. I always lock the door."

Ben looked to Gary for help. "You can do this," Gary told him.

"You broke in," Martha added.

"Nothing's broken," Ben said quickly. "The door, it really was open. I didn't even touch it."

She turned her head to look at him, and noticed the Scythe hanging overhead. "Some doors aren't meant to open," she growled. "Get out. Now." She climbed slowly to her feet, bony hand grabbing the glass beside her. The water spilled onto the floor.

Ben edged out of the kitchen backwards. Gary placed a hand on his shoulder, keeping his distance from Martha as she advanced on them. Ben estimated her to be in her eighties. She was shorter than him, more so when she leaned over, but with her hair falling loosely over her face, a toothy snarl on her face and a fire in her eyes, she was more menacing than any old lady he'd ever met.

He almost paused. That fire in her eyes wasn't just a trick of the light.

Gary pushed down on Ben's shoulder roughly, forcing him to his hunkers as the glass flew from Martha's hand. It soared over their heads, coated in a bright orange flame. When the glass smashed against the floor, fire spilled up onto the door. The old woman screamed, and the door slammed shut. Where her eyes should have been, there was only fire, fire that spread to every item she could get her hands on. A burning clock sent her magazine pile scattering, flames showering the carpet.

In the middle of the ruckus, Ben and Gary became separated.

The Reaper-in-Training remained Martha's primary target. She threw whatever she could get her bony hands on in his direction. Her curtains burned at the hands of a flaming family photograph. Her mouldy couch became a bonfire when Ben ducked beneath a china plate.

The Scythe sang to the destruction, and Ben could only keep his distance. She had him cornered, now; the door was a death-trap, the window a ring of fire, the stairs catching alight just as he neared them, and the rest of the room burning up quickly. Smoke was swimming around his head, and he began to choke.

"Some doors aren't meant to open," she said to him, "but I'm sure they won't mind taking you in my place." She raised her arms over her head, another plate ready to burn, and only one place to throw it.

A flash of light from her back caused her to freeze on the spot. Through the smoke, Ben could see Gary, hand outstretched and placed against the old woman.

"Use the Scythe, Ben," he shouted.

The blade glowed in response to Gary's words, and Ben felt his arm rise of its own volition. The tip of the Scythe touched against Martha's chest. In an instant, the fire in her eyes dimmed to darkness, her regular eyes reappearing as if from behind a veil of darkness. A soft light spilled from the contact point with the Scythe, blue with a thread of red weaving through it like a serpent. It seemed to empty her, leaving a frail old woman collapsing into Gary's arms.

The former-Reaper closed his eyes and released a slow, steady breath. All at once, the fires in the room began to dwindle away to nothingness, leaving sorry scorch marks all over the house. He passed Martha over to Ben, and raised his arms over his head, a pale light forming in his palms. With a clap and a burst of light, he set a series of actions into motion. The curtains hung themselves back up, stitching themselves back together. The wood in the door began to fill up with ash and solidify again. The carpet rolled out over the gaps that had been burnt away. The magazines restacked themselves, the glass zipped back to the kitchen, the china plates un-smashing, and the couch remoulding itself.

By the time the room was repaired, Martha had stopped breathing.

"What was that?" Ben asked.

"That was step four," Gary responded. He helped Ben move Martha onto the couch. "A little clean-up. It's something I picked up over the years. Once you've made a proper connection to the Scythe, you'll find that you can perform certain magical feats." He led Ben back to the kitchen and sat down in the chair. Black rings had formed under his eyes.

"Are you okay?"

"I'll live. I just didn't expect that for your first case. She should have been an easier one." He took a few deep breaths, his eyes closed. Ben did that when he was trying to stop the room spinning after a few too many drinks. "She's what happens when a corrupted soul isn't removed quickly enough. The world is a little more fragile than we like to believe. Magics seep through the fabric of reality."

Ben looked out at Martha, lying completely still on the couch. "She was lonely," he said. "She needed company. She needed her family."

Gary nodded. "Now you're getting it. Everyone needs somebody. She was still looking for that. Sometimes, a goodbye is all people need to let go. Without it, there's no telling what will happen." Colour began returning to his face, and he stood up to join Ben at the doorway. "They're usually simpler than that. Unwilling, but not corrupted. The soul is a strange thing." He placed a hand on Ben's shoulder. "Now, step five."

Ben looked at the Scythe in his hand. He couldn't remember putting it down to help Martha, nor could he remember picking it back up again. It felt natural in his hand already. He wasn't sure that was such a good thing. The Scythe chimed back its opinion of him. He still didn't know what it meant.

"What happened to the soul?" he asked Gary. "What did the Scythe do with it?"

"In the right hands, it takes a soul and stores it away for transportation. A Scythe is extradimensional in nature. It extends beyond what we can see. It's one of the few things in existence that can touch a human soul. It pulls them out, and keeps them safe. Once inside a Scythe, a soul only has one destination. Headquarters, to be sent onwards to the great Beyond."

The words meant nothing to Ben. It wasn't his reality. It wasn't his religion. Beyond? That was just another word for Heaven, as far as he was concerned. He closed his eyes, listening to the singing of the Scythe in his hand. He asked it to help, to send Martha's soul where it needed to go. For a moment, the Scythe seemed to hesitate.

"It'll help Gary. It'll give him the peace he needs to start over," Ben thought to himself. He hoped the Scythe would hear him, as worried as he was to have this incomprehensible object reaching about inside his mind.

It sang back its response, and the blade glowed red once more.

"Well done, Ben," Gary said to him. "Your first case, handled like a pro. I hope you're ready for your next one." Out of nowhere, he pulled another folder. "I have to go to Headquarters. They want me to report back on how you did. Professional opinion, and all that. For the next couple of weeks, until you've found your feet, I'm your supervisor. Then I'm out of the business altogether."

Ben skimmed through the folder. "Is this serious?"

"It's an old case. One we've been struggling with for a while. It's not dangerous. It's not like this one." Gary looked to the Scythe. "Trust your instincts, even those that make you feel at odds with yourself. The Scythe knows what it's doing. Research your case, then act. I'll find you later."

Paul Carroll

Chapter Three: The Necromancer's Debt

No matter one's circumstances in life, so long as one remained in control of themselves and made their own decisions, things were a little less scary. Unfortunately for Ben Cooper, no one told the Scythe that he was the master, and it was the tool. When Gary disappeared in a burst of light, the Scythe saw fit to get Ben started on his research. Almost immediately, he found himself staring at the young man from the folder that Gary had handed him.

The words *Living Memories* sang in his head; he got the impression that the Scythe wouldn't always speak to him like that. The photograph of the man began to move, and Ben was forced to follow him as if he were the cameraman in a silent movie. He followed him through cobbled streets, staring at the back of his head as he marched on casually and confidently towards a building labelled BANK. The man was dressed in a smart suit, with a swagger to his step. The people around him looked miserable, sick even. Ben counted half a dozen children without shoes. Half of them were crying. Their parents were trying to draw their attention away from the man in the suit.

The story began to tell itself to Ben.

His name was Arnold Schultz. He was born in 1857 in Germany to humble farming parents. His father died in 1882, but continued working on the family farm for a further twenty years. In those years, he didn't age a day. He barely ate. He couldn't sleep. And he refused to talk to a priest.

Arnold had done something to his father, and everyone feared it.

In 1892, Arnold also figured out how to stop himself and his mother aging. She was, at this point, feeling weary from age. After Arnold, she had been incapable of having more children. When her husband's body finally fell apart, when she was a sixty-one-year-old woman in a fifty-one-year-old woman's body, she tried to hang herself.

She hung by her neck for three days while Arnold was away on business, building himself a secret fortune, doing the work that everyone in their small town was too afraid to talk about. Outraged at her decision, Arnold destroyed their home, with her still inside. This one action, more than anything else he had done, alerted the Reapers to something otherworldly in Europe. There was a rogue necromancer playing God, and he had to be stopped.

It took the first Reaper three years to find Arnold. At this point, he had crossed the Atlantic and was living in Boston. European politics was becoming disturbingly fraught, and rather than keep himself in the middle of what looked to be an impending war zone, he emigrated. He kept his name, but forged his papers. When questioned about his business in the United States, Arnold stated, "Pleasure." The word rang in Ben's head.

The scene continued to unfold. Arnold Schultz approached a bank in Boston in 1907 to open an account. Ben watched him pull an absurd amount of gold from the inner pockets of his jacket, though the teller seemed unfazed by the odd display. His age was more unsettling for the teller; Arnold had the appearance of a twenty-five-year-old, the wealth of a man at least a decade older, and none of the usual titles and authority that came with such a fortune.

The Scythe sang in Ben's ears, and the scene froze. Arnold took on a red hue and continued moving about the bank, suddenly aware that something was different. Ben's attention was caught by another man glowing red at the entrance to the bank, a long Scythe in his right hand, and a horrid black robe covering his skeletal body.

"That's new," Arnold said in amusement. He spoke with a clear American accent, all traces of his home gone from his voice. He took in the sight of the Reaper with a smirk on his face. "You're not one of mine. Who brought you back?" The Reaper shook his head. "No, not back. You're still alive in there, under all that smoke and shadow. Who are you? What did you do to these people?"

The eyes of the Reaper burned brightly when he spoke. "I am one of the Seven, tasked with collecting where a debt is due. I am a Reaper, charged with protecting the natural world from the influence of corrupted souls."

Arnold paced back and forth, considering the Reaper's words. "My soul is fine. My mother's was released when she died. You're not the only one who knows a thing or two about them." He let out a laugh. "You're scared of me, aren't you? You and yours, you're afraid that I'm going to put you out of business."

The Reaper ignored his jests. "I have been charged with ending this charade of yours. Your body is an unnatural cage to your soul."

Arnold patted himself down. "I'm young. I'm relatively fit, if a bit on the skinny side. You can blame my parents for that. But there are no signs of corruption here. There's no danger of my body failing me. There's nothing you can say to convince me that you're right."

"Then allow my Scythe to speak for me," the Reaper said quietly, and dashed forwards without a sound, blade shining blindingly. He brought it down at Arnold, aiming for his chest with more ferocity than Ben was aware a skeleton could display.

Suffice to say, the Reaper missed. Arnold was, as suddenly as the Reaper had leapt at him, standing behind his grim opponent. He tugged roughly at the robes, forcing the Reaper to the ground, and wrapped his hand around the handle of the Scythe. He let go after a few seconds, leaving the Reaper stunned and silent.

"It's an interesting weapon you have there," Arnold observed. "And no more shall you bring it near me." He clapped his hands together, and a series of incomprehensible glyphs shone around the Reaper. The Scythe vanished, and the uniform pealed itself from the Reaper's body. The man left kneeling on the floor of the bank began to whimper. Arnold ignored his pleas for mercy. With a click of his fingers, the Reaper was covered in a burning light, and disappeared.

Ben suddenly found himself in a hospital, where the Reaper was strapped to a bed. He screamed nonsense into an otherwise empty room, and the Scythe sang softly for him as the scene faded.

Ben reappeared next to the body of Martha Underwood. She looked peaceful and quiet. Not at all like the Reaper that, Ben understood, had once held the very Scythe that Gary had passed on to him.

"Arnold Schultz drove him mad?" Ben asked the Scythe. It seemed to chime a positive response. "And made it so you couldn't get near him again?" He paused, wondering why Gary would give him such an impossible case. He opened up the file, looking for further help with the necromancer.

His charges were listed plainly and simply: undercharging for his services, since the 1907 Bank Affair; refusing to allow his body to die, thereby threatening the value of his soul to the Beyond; creating additional work for Reaper HQ with each recovered soul from the Beyond; ensuring an imbalance in the universe through a long history of necromancy on a global level, and; fraternising with a potential threat to the universe.

It made Ben's head spin.

Beneath Arnold's crimes, there were but a few solutions listed: convince him to give up his body, convince him to raise his prices, and convince him to give up the location of a person whose name had since been redacted from the file. Ben tried not to worry about that one.

A century-long list of Reapers who had attempted to complete the Arnold Schultz case had been signed off on the last page of the file, after a few hundred pages of detailed accounts of Schultz's necromancy throughout his 160-year lifetime. There were a dozen names on the list, and right at the bottom, dated in 2003, was Gary Murphy. Every Reaper who had gone up against Arnold had failed. Ben was just relieved to see that they hadn't necessarily been killed by him. Gary was living proof of that.

"So what do we do?" Ben asked the Scythe. "Do you know where he is?"

He wished he hadn't said anything. Rather than simply tell him, the Scythe teleported them across the country, dropping him roughly in a graveyard. He brushed himself off, fighting a chill in the air. His sweater wasn't doing him much good against the wind, but he had bigger issues to contend with. He could see Arnold in the middle of a lightshow across the graveyard, standing with a couple underneath an incredibly worried-looking apple tree.

Ben hurried as fast as his legs would allow him to. The Scythe hid itself from view, but he could feel its presence at the back of his head. It urged him onwards, but with caution, a sensation he wasn't used to feeling from the tool that had so far mostly refused to co-operate with him.

He stopped a few feet from the scene. "Arnold," he said quietly. His tongue felt numb when he tried to speak, and he found it moving by itself, lips sounding out words as required. The Scythe sang in his ear, and he could see vague memories of a younger Gary Murphy approaching Arnold

Schultz. He tried to stay calm. "You broke the tree," he told the necromancer.

Both the leaves and the apples on the tree turned completely black, while its bark turned a stark white. Ben wasn't aware of any apple tree that had fruit at this time of the year, but he wasn't about to question anything with the necromancer standing in front of him.

"I'm here to collect," he told Arnold. "A life for a life."

The Scythe flickered into existence in Ben's hand, but as far as he could tell, the woman standing nearby couldn't see it. The man beside her smirked, and the Scythe sang in Ben's head to indicate that he was, despite all appearances, Arnold Schultz.

"And the body you were promised," Arnold told him, eyeing the Scythe with a grin on his face. The Scythe showed Ben a memory of Gary, talking to the necromancer all those years ago.

"A deal is a deal. One more time, and I had to collect. You owed a debt." Gary had made him agree on a quota. Despite everything that had happened, despite Gary's apparent failure, he had given Ben a chance at putting an end to the necromancer's trouble.

The Scythe glowed in Ben's hand, and the body of Arnold Schultz collapsed to the ground. The woman screamed, though Ben wasn't aware of any reason why the death of Arnold's original body was of concern to her.

The necromancer smiled at Ben from beside her. There was no denying it. Within his eyes, Ben could see the very essence of his soul, the man who had bested a Reaper over a hundred years ago. Whatever he had done, he had made sure to stick to Gary's deal. The body was dead, as HQ had requested, and Arnold's soul seemed intact.

"And now that we've all paid…" Arnold said.

The Scythe pulled Ben away from the scene as quickly as it could. He could feel its panic, its worries, and its relief.

They landed at the edge of the graveyard, and Ben's tongue came loose again.

"We did it," he said to the Scythe. "Well... you did it. You and Gary." The Scythe shimmered in his hand, blinking out of sight. He looked around for it, and found Arnold Schultz behind him.

"I should have switched bodies years ago," he said triumphantly. "You forget how it feels to truly be alive when you stay the same for so long. Not that you'd know anything about that." He draped a heavy arm over Ben's shoulders. "You're new. Gary's replacement, I'm assuming. Your Scythe and I, we have a bit of a history." He gave Ben a tight squeeze. "My name is Arnold. This body is Mattie Brown. He wasn't ready to come back. A lot of them aren't."

He guided Ben around the graveyard, keeping him close. Ben wasn't sure if it was meant to be an intimidation technique, or if he was simply attempting to make conversation. At the bank, he had been a wiry, wild character. Oozing in confidence, despite himself. Mattie had taken care of himself when he was alive. Mattie was taller and stronger, and Arnold seemed proud of himself for having taken over the body when he did.

"This is the part where you introduce yourself," Arnold told him. "Gary and I, we had a deal. I'd make a few more deals, and then I had to give myself up. Do you have any idea how selective I've had to be with my work?" Ben shook his head. "No, I suppose not. Name. Now."

The Scythe chimed at the back of Ben's head. "Ben Cooper," he said quickly. "Gary's replacement, yeah. He... I guess, he quit."

Arnold laughed, and then stopped himself. "So that's how this body does that," he mused. "Gary was always a bit sensitive. When I met him, he looked at meat sacks like they were the important part in all of this. I bet it was the damn ape last year that really did it for him." He ran a hand through his hair. "But you know, meat sacks are good. A soul can't stay alive without one. I wouldn't be able to keep doing what I do without a body to do it in."

"Is that why you stole that one?" Ben asked him.

Arnold stopped them walking and grabbed Ben roughly by the collar. "I had a deal with that lady," he snarled. "I don't steal."

The Scythe was silent. Ben really wished that it would do something, that it would take him out of the graveyard. It felt him to stand there, gulping at the very presence of the newly improved Arnold Schultz. The necromancer glared at him for a moment, maintaining eye contact, before he finally started to laugh.

"Oh man, you are way too uptight," he cheered. He let go of Ben's sweater. "I'm not going to hurt you kid. It's not my game. But I will warn you: don't take up the Scythe." Ben waited for him to laugh, but it didn't come. "I've met a lot of Reapers in my time, first at the bank and then every few years since. Most came to try kill me. None of them lasted long, anyway. That job of yours, it changes people. Make sure you know who you want to be before you head down this path."

He left Ben standing in the graveyard. Arnold didn't need to teleport away to avoid questions. He didn't need to warn Ben not to follow him. He simply turned his back on him and walked away, a swagger in his step and Mattie Brown's best suit on his back.

The Cooper kitchen was sparkling when Ben arrived home. If not for the bag of cans by the back door and the basket of empty bottles beside it, away from the neighbourhood cats, the damage of the night before would have been nothing but a distant memory. He found his phone charging on the worktop, only registering then that he hadn't had it with him all day. He checked the date; still January 1st.

"You're home," Jean said to him. She stood with a cup of tea by the door to the kitchen. "We were all kind of worried that we wouldn't get to see you again." Macy shuffled into the room, pawing at Ben's legs. Jean just smiled at her, barely making eye contact with her brother. She was biting her lip softly.

"You're not asking me something," he said to her. "You do that lip-bite thing when you want to ask something. You did it all the time when we were kids."

Her face turned red. "Okay, yeah. I guess. What was it like?"

Ben didn't know how much to tell her. He didn't know how much he *could* tell her. He was sure there were some rules they hadn't mentioned to him about what sort of information was private, and what sort of stuff was best left a secret.

"An old lady tried to kill me," he blurted out.

She laughed. She couldn't help it. "You're going to need to expand on that one."

So, he told her. He told her what he knew about souls. He told her what he knew about necromancers. He tried not to explain too much about the Scythe, when it made complaints in the back of his mind about being talked about. She asked about Gary, and he gave her the full story of Arnold Schultz.

When he finished, she pulled him into a hug. "What was that for?" he asked.

"I'm just really glad that you found something you're enthusiastic about," she told him, and left him to ponder his thoughts.

Maybe he had been a bit excited to tell her about his day. Maybe he had enjoyed it, when he wasn't being used for target practice. And, maybe, he even liked having the Scythe with him. Macy eyed him jealously, and he knelt down beside her. "No one can replace you, girl."

Macy sat at the end of his bed that night. He tried not to think about Arnold's warning as he drifted off, a wild party and the first day of the weirdest job on the planet finally taking their toll on him.

Chapter Four: Apocalypse Soon-ish

Ben was not the best at recognising towns based on their architecture. He guessed he was still in America. He knew he wasn't in a major city. But that was about as far as he could get in his deductions. He stood at a crossroads, waiting. There was no traffic. He was aware that there were people around him. He shied away from looking at them. There was something more important grabbing his attention.

The sky. His gaze was drawn upwards to it. There was a crack, spilling out thick black fog like storm clouds. With a boom, the crack grew, tearing half-way to the horizon. It was jagged and uneven, splintering outwards in every direction, a vacuous black stain overhead.

Then, a light. A pinprick, really, and the first of many thousands. Ben stared at them as they began to grow. He had a niggling suspicion that they were moving quickly in his direction. When they began to burst through the tear, he wished more than anything that he could get his feet to move. The light came from white-hot fireballs, each one burning through the atmosphere leaving a dirty trail in its wake.

When they came closer, he could hear them. They were screaming, deeply human cries for help. His arms refused to move, no matter how much he tried to cover his ears against the noise.

The Beyond, a voice told him. The Scythe

He stared into the darkness, and it stared back. These weren't just fireballs descending from the sky. They were souls. He could feel them calling out to him, the Reaper who should be saving them. The Reaper whose job it was to protect the souls of all humankind. What was he doing now, but standing there while they fell? What was he doing to stop this?

He forced his eyes away from the falling souls. They were a few minutes from impact, he thought. His eyes rested on the nearby buildings, which were suddenly finding themselves cracking under the pressure of the tear in the sky. In some places, the stonework crumbled into a rising column, drawn towards to the Beyond. In other places, the walls were breaking down into a heavy pile of stone and steel, bending and twisting, grinding as it resisted destruction. The roads were breaking up, in some places collapsing through into the sewers, in others drifting upwards.

The unsettling of gravity all around him made Ben's stomach lurch. His footing was uncertain, and he couldn't tell if or when he'd be swimming through the air into the darkness beyond the falling fog, if he could avoid the burning souls as they made their way back to Earth.

Fresh screams reached his ears, and he became aware of the civilians all around him. Men and women were fighting with each other, punching and biting and kicking whenever they could. They smashed windows of stores, pulling televisions out through shattered glass, filling bags with groceries, emptying cash registers or simply taking them with them to deal with later. Children's cries were piercing the violence. Ben tried not to look for them. He couldn't bear the thought of it, never mind the reality.

In his efforts to avoid looking at the riots, he became aware of the appearance of other Reapers, each dressed in their uniforms. Five skeletal faces looked ahead, unmoving and unflinching; they bore their Scythes in their best hands, each one slightly different in shape, and with blades glowing along a spectrum of colours. A deep, sea blue; an emerald green; a fiery orange; a golden yellow, and; a rose pink.

The Reapers surrounded him, and he followed their line of sight. He almost wished he hadn't. At the very last second, he caught sight of another Scythe, a deep purple glow swinging for his head, and a twisted, inhuman laugh ringing in his ears.

Ben fell out of bed, crashing painfully onto the shoes he'd worn yesterday. Macy leapt up in shock and began barking. Ben's first instinct was to quieten the dog, calling her over in hushed tones. "It's okay," he told her, "Go back to sleep." Macy lay down beside him, but he wasn't sure she'd actually fall sleep now. Neither was he, with his heart pounding the way it was. His head hurt, and he could still hear the laughter echoing at the back of his mind. The Scythe sang over it, and he wished that he could see it. It popped into his hand, helping him prop himself up from the floor.

Ben had never considered his Scythe to be part of a set, but the blood red glow matched the others he had seen in his dream. It hadn't felt like any dream he'd had before, but he had no other word for it.

"I don't suppose you saw any of that?" he asked the Scythe. The blade remained silent. "No, I guess not. You're not *that* invasive, are you?" He checked his phone. January 2nd, and four-thirty in the morning. Too early to get up, and too late to try get back to sleep. He resolved to dressing just enough to sit downstairs without a chill setting in.

The kitchen lights were already on when Ben entered the room. Martin sat at the table, a half-empty glass of water in front of him. He didn't notice Ben walking in. "You're up early," Ben said to him quietly. He sat down beside his father. He hadn't had the chance to talk to him since Gary's arrival the morning before.

Martin played with the glass, lifting it to his mouth, but pausing before taking a sip. "I couldn't sleep," he muttered.

"Something on your mind?"

Martin shook his head. "Compared to every other night of my life, I think I'm good. Your mother and I, we spent half our lives waiting for someone to show up on our door like that. For the first night in my life, I'm not worrying about whether tomorrow will be the day I'm going to have to say goodbye to my wife and kids." He drained his glass in one gulp. "Fancy making tea?" Ben nodded, unsure how else to respond. "And hey, while you're up, turn the heating on."

"Seriously?"

"I think it's about time this house had some warmth in it. Maybe your mother will sleep a little bit better from now on."

They were quiet while the kettle boiled, a deafening roar against the silence of the house, fighting the pipes for whatever might wake Amanda and Jean from their sleep. Ben was surprised that the heaters still worked. His grandmother had always told him to count his blessings, so he kept his mouth shut on the matter.

"I'm sorry about what happened yesterday," Martin told him as he placed their cups on the table. "We never thought…"

Ben hushed him. "It's better this way," he said firmly. "Some people might say it's too early to really judge this, but I'd prefer have this weird job and this strange life than lose you like that." He heard the Scythe in the back of his mind, and did his best to ignore it. "Mom and Jean need you here more than they need me to have a real job, anyway."

The Scythe sang louder in the back of his mind, a whistle unlike anything he'd heard from it so far. He was stuck for its meaning, but it was beginning to distract him from the moment.

Martin took notice of his sudden shift in behaviour. "Are you okay, son?"

Ben's hands began to tremble, and he quickly hid them under the table. "Headache. Just a sudden headache." However much he could tell Jean, there were limits to the sort of conversations he could have with his parents. He and Jean, they were always there for each other. But there had always been that suspicion that their parents were keeping something from them, and Gary's arrival yesterday brought out that truth more suddenly than any of them had been ready for. Ben knew he'd have to tell them about the Scythe, sooner rather than later, and maybe tell them about the likes of Mrs Underwood and Arnold Schultz.

While he was still figuring it all out, he knew that he couldn't talk about it with them. A headache was as good an excuse as he might need to provide. He imagined himself saying 'Duty calls' a few times, too, over the course of his private life within the Death Business, when the conversation would be too difficult or too complicated.

"Try get some rest," Martin said simply, visibly holding back the questions that were on the tip of his tongue.

Ben left him sitting there, grateful for the permission to leave, and almost pleased that they had a shared understanding of their relationship. But 'almost' was never quite enough

He hadn't lied about the headache. The Scythe continued screaming in his head for another couple of hours, when he decided that showering and dressing for the day might serve as a better alternative to going stir crazy in his bed with a snoring Macy by his side. He barely had his shoes tied when his phone rang. No one called Ben this early in the morning.

Few people called him normally, unless they were old friends back in town for the weekend.

He didn't recognise the number. "Hello?" he said quietly. He hoped he was speaking quietly. The Scythe was drowning out almost all over noise.

"You need to talk," a voice said. The Scythe immediately quietened down. Gary. He beat Ben to the question. "I've got a couple of weeks to train you in to some degree of competency, before I retire and you're on your own with the other Reapers. The Scythe can still reach me to some degree, until HQ officially closes the book on me. Meet me there as soon as you can, and we can figure something out that doesn't have us both up for hours."

"Wait, how do I–" Gary hung up. "Get to HQ…" The Scythe chimed in his head, and Ben gulped. He didn't like where this was going, and found himself violently thrown onto the cold, white floor of an unfamiliar office.

Some would say that the room was well lit; Ben would argue that the volume and intensity of the lights in the room were verging on blinding. He squinted through tired eyes as dozens of people rushed by him on every side, each carrying folders and/or clipboards, dressed in immaculate light or grey suits. Their hair was always neat, their posture almost perfect, their shoes shining and pristine, and their faces as practically devoid of emotion. Men and women alike ignored him as they went about their day, either oblivious to his sudden appearance, or – the more likely scenario, as far as Ben was concerned – entirely apathetic.

A tall desk was positioned in the centre of the room, occupied by two clerks. One, a woman, had almost bleached-blonde hair, silver lipstick and the palest complexion Ben had ever laid eyes on. She wore a shimmering grey suit, just dull enough to look formal, and just dazzling enough to fit into her aesthetic. Beside her, a man was dressed in an entirely plain grey suit, with a crop of brown hair on his head; even reduced to the minimal facial expressions that seemed fitting of the office, to Ben he looked utterly depressed at his station. Like everyone else in the office, they kept their eyes off the latest arrival.

Ben eased his way across the room, weaving between the continuous line of administrative staff that rushed in every direction. He stopped next to a map of the world, fingers tracing across pinpoints all over the world. Thousands of them filled the map, spread unevenly across every continent. There was a focus of them in major cities, and with a few locations otherwise outshining the rest.

"There's no official term for them," Gary told him. The man stepped up beside Ben, tired eyes and a half smile upon his face. "I call them Flight Risks, but it's always been a bit of a misnomer. They're the ones who are likely to stay, rather than go. They're what keep Reapers busy throughout the year."

Ben couldn't count them. Even New York looked like too much work for one person. "How do you know which ones are Flight Risks?" he asked.

"Sometimes, they demonstrate a particular fondness for life. The ones who rarely give in when all the odds are against them, the ones who can't let go of a relationship that's fallen apart, the ones who hate to lose, they're the ones who keep themselves anchored to the world. A Reaper sets them free from their earthly ties, before they do anyone any harm. The longer a soul stays after death, the more volatile it becomes."

"Then, there are those who are surrounded by those who love too deeply. When a Reaper visits them, a simple conversation won't do. The Scythe is required, always. Other people keep them bound to the Earth, whether they know it or not."

Ben pointed out some of the more rural areas, where there were more lights shining than even some of the larger cities and towns. "What about them?"

Gary ran his finger across the map, joining two of the rural points together. "Some people believe it has something to do with ley lines, but even up here the science is a little…uncertain. Most of these places were important for spiritual reasons. Some of them are sites of mass-murder. There's a certain energy where spirituality and death are concerned that sometimes serves to tie souls to the mortal world more commonly than in most places. A simple community church, even the Vatican, isn't imbued with such power. Ancient traditions are more dangerous; some of them came with real power, the sort no one believes in anymore."

He took Ben by the shoulders and steered him from the map before he could ask any more questions. Doing so only pointed the young Reaper towards a People of Interest board. Gary groaned when Ben moved towards it.

There were only a few people on the board. One was missing a face, as if it had been wiped away altogether. His hair was changing colour as Ben watched, shifting between every natural hue in a repeating cycle.

Next to him, a familiar face. Ben almost laughed. Arnold Schultz, his old face on display for the whole room. He wondered if they were behind on their administrative work, or if they simply hadn't realised that Ben had done what no one else before him had managed, with a lot of help from Gary. The picture of Arnold was identical to the photograph that had been in his file, which Ben began to realise had been cropped from a larger picture.

Beside Arnold, a woman. Her hair was barely contained by a combination of derby hat and a hair tie. She was smiling for the camera; Ben had the impression that she had dressed for the picture specifically. He wasn't sure who she was, or what she was doing on the board, and he wasn't sure Gary was going to tell him.

Beneath them, another line of photos showed even less about the people in them. There was a man with his hand covering his face, sitting in a small booth with a crystal ball and deck of tarot cards beside him on a table. Next to him was the back of someone's head, everything about them completely concealed by the poor angle of the photograph. Next to that person, was a collage of crime-scene-photos, instead of a headshot. Ben moved closer, against Gary's wishes; bodies, dozens of them, all with bloodied necks and pale faces.

"A vampire," Gary told him. "A clever one, too. No one's tracked him or her down, yet."

"Who are all these people?" Ben asked.

Gary sighed. "It's too much for your second day. They're important. Strange things happen in the world; sometimes they're more violent than we're used to, and sometimes they're just downright bizarre. Each of the seven individuals on that board fall into one or both of those categories. You'll learn more, eventually."

Ben frowned, catching a glimpse of the final picture before – with a swipe of Gary's hand – the board was removed from view: a child, maybe nine or ten, staring directly at the camera.

"I can handle it," Ben argued.

"You woke up with something on your mind," Gary reminded him. "I think it's about time you told me about it. And, HR. Also a misnomer, given the staff here, but you understand the term."

Ben knew that he was right. Of course he was. He had more experience in the business of being a Reaper than Ben had at being a functioning adult. He allowed Gary to lead him across the room, pausing with everyone else when a set of double doors opened.

From them, a man stepped through. His skin was black as coal and looked smooth to the touch, as if he had been carved out of stone. He looked down upon everyone in the room, at least seven-foot-tall by Ben's judgement, wearing a glistening silver suit. His hair was pure white and slicked backwards, just long enough to reach halfway down his neck.

His eyes sent chills up Ben's spine. Where they should have been, were sparks of glowing white lightning, the same way a Reaper's eyes were when they were in uniform. Ben wondered if he should have been dressed for the job, the way the man looked at him.

Ben opened his mouth to speak, but the Scythe sent a warning note through his head. He almost flinched at the volume of it.

"If you would, the records you were requesting are through here," a short lady told the man. He nodded, following her out of the lobby. On cue, everyone's shoulders slumped.

"Who was that guy?" Ben whispered.

"That was no 'guy'. That was the angel Kerubiel, Regent of the Cherubim." Gary took a few deep breaths. "I didn't know he was due for a visit today, or I wouldn't have told you to come here. Angels are tricky beings to deal with. The folklore around them can be difficult to understand, and it's impossible to apply. Translation has made them foreign to us, and they rarely speak directly to the people who work here. Kerubiel is one of the few actual visitors to the offices."

Ben wanted to let that settle in his mind, but a question was escaping his mouth before he knew he was ready for the answer. "So, Christians are right?"

Gary laughed. "It's impossible to answer that, too. The closest you'll ever get to a divine Being is an angel, and they're not the chattiest. They'd never disclose the truth." He could see the disappointment on Ben's face, and leaned in close. "But here's a trade secret," he whispered. "As far as we know, with as much evidence as we've been able to acquire off the record, whatever exists Beyond is open to a lot more interpretation than most people would willingly believe until they die."

The Scythe whistled in his ears, teasingly. It figured to Ben that, maybe, the Scythe knew more than it would ever tell him. Someone had to create it. Someone had to introduce the Reapers to the world. Someone, or something. Following that logic, the Scythe might know the truth, the whole truth of creation, of the divine. And, in a manner completely befitting the all-too-sentient tool of his trade, it kept its proverbial lips sealed on the subject.

Gary clapped him on the shoulder. "Try not to think about it, too much," he said in jest. "Now, onto HR." He brought Ben up to the desk, where the mismatched pair sat. The man was close to tears, and the woman's smile looked ready to tear through her face. "You knew he was coming," Gary observed. "Kudos on restraining the fangirling. Could you tell Becky I'll be up to her?"

"Sure thing, Gar," the woman chirped.

Gary led Ben into an elevator; Kerubiel had gone through the same doors, but the elevator looked too small to contain the angel. Ben repeated Gary's advice to himself in his head, doing his best to push the idea of the angel out of his mind before he gave himself an aneurysm.

There were no buttons in the elevator, which troubled Ben to no end, but when the doors opened again, Gary seemed satisfied that they were on the right floor. Instead of white tiles and blinding lights, they walked across large stone tiles through what could only be described as a jungle, complete with a stream running along the path. Birds chirped within the leaves, but none showed themselves to the visitors.

In the middle of the room, where the stream met several others, was a pool of water. In its centre was a desk, fashioned to look like the trees, with two chairs on one side and a woman sitting in a third on the far side. She shot a half smile in their direction as they approached.

"Gary, my dear," she announced, standing up for them. "I was so sad to get your letter of resignation. Come, come, have a seat." The pool of water parted as they walked through it, leaving them bone-dry. Ben added it to the list of things to ignore for the time being.

The woman, Becky, was taller than Gary, dressed in a dark blue skirted-suit. Her hair was tinted evergreen, pinned up out of her face. Her eyes were distinctly different colours, one deep blue, the other a lush green. When she clasped her hands in front of her, Ben counted seven fingers on each one, thumbs included. He thought about what Gary had said about misnomers, but figured it would be impolite to ask what Becky was.

"You must be Benjamin Cooper," she said to him firmly. "Gary called me. You're having trouble on the job?"

Ben shook his head. Gary coughed, urging him to speak up. "Yesterday was okay. I think it went well. I mean, I only have... I don't know... normal, boring jobs to compare it to, but..."

She rapped her fingers against the table. "No 'buts', Mister Cooper. Not in your profession. You must be certain, do you understand? Just some helpful advice."

He nodded, looking to Gary for support. His supervisor had his eyes trained on Becky, and the Scythe was likewise quiet. "I met Arnold Schultz yesterday," Ben told her. "I think... I mean, the Scythe assured me that the case was closed, now."

Becky smiled widely to Gary. "See? Nothing to worry about."

"I suppose," Gary said quietly.

Becky stood up to usher them out, but Ben stuck up a hand. "Actually, that's not that was bothering me." She looked to him suspiciously, and Gary sneered when she wasn't looking. "I had a dream last night, but it didn't feel like a dream. It felt real, and it was sort of…end of the world-y?"

He mentioned the other Reapers, the tear in the sky, and the riots, but Becky was nonplussed about his story. "Dreams happen," she told him. "Do you have any experience with prophetic visions?" Ben shook his head. "What about extradimensional perception?" Again, he shook his head. "And I'm assuming you are not related to the Fates of old lore. It was just a dream."

"Are you sure?" Gary asked her.

"It is neither his job, nor yours, to worry about these things," Becky replied. She produced a file from under her desk, identical on the outside to the files that Gary had given Ben the day previous. "Reap souls, and leave the maintenance of the universe to the professionals in this building."

With that, she sat down, ushering them out of her office and back onto the elevator. The moment the doors closed, Gary pulled Ben close. "I'll look into it, if you want," he whispered. "Something in your story doesn't add up, and I intend to figure it out. In the meantime, do your job, and keep your head down. For your dad's sake." Ben nodded, losing Gary to a flash of light the moment the doors opened at the lobby.

"For dad," he muttered to himself.

Paul Carroll

CHAPTER FIVE: THE UNDYING GIRL

The list of things that Ben decided should not be immediately questioned was growing as his time with the Scythe grew. He summed it up so far, taking into account that it wasn't yet nine in the morning on his second day of work:

- Divine Beings, and whether they existed;
- Dreams, insofar as he was unqualified to have them;
- The multiple non-human species working at the Reaper HQ;
- The purpose of all the administrative staff at said HQ;
- The role of angels;
- What would happen if he spoke to an angel;
- What would happen if an angel spoke to him;
- How a whole jungle fit inside the building;
- Where the building was physically positioned;
- What really happened to souls when they were removed from bodies, and;
- How the files of soon-to-be-Reaped souls updated themselves.

The latter was of primary concern to him as he sat in a chair in the lobby reading through the file.

The woman's name was Lydia May. She was twenty-three years old, she was dying, and unwilling to go quietly. The words wrote themselves, quite literally, as Ben was reading them. Her photograph was materialising as he stared at the page. There wasn't much to go on. No cause of death.

No job. No next-of-kin. No other details but her address, an apartment in the Bronx.

Despite its habit of hiding from plain view, the Scythe stayed true to fashion and dragged Ben from his seat in the lobby to Lydia's front door. He had little time to complain, stumbling from the sudden jump through space and landing square against her door. He up-righted himself just in time before she opened her door.

Ben could describe Lydia May in three ways, the first time he met her: from appearances, completely healthy; at a quick glance, mostly naked from the waist down, but her for her underwear, and; more annoyed than he had ever seen a woman look, most likely a result of having been disturbed so early in the morning by a stranger crashing against her door.

His heart skipped a beat, and for a brief moment he wondered how that would feel if he were in uniform.

"What do you want?" she asked him. He stared back her blankly. "Buddy, what are you selling?" He shook his head, his mouth refusing to speak the words that he thought were needed. He had no idea how to even begin the conversation with Lydia. Her face softened almost immediately. "Are you okay? Do you need a glass of water?" He nodded, but didn't move. Lydia did the only thing that, Ben assumed, made sense to her, and pulled him forcefully inside by his sweater. "Sit down over there. I'll be back in a minute with some pants and a glass of water."

"I'm already wearing pants," Ben mumbled.

"And I'm really happy for both of us that you are, but they're for me." She stormed out of the room, leaving Ben by the door. "The boiler in the building is on the fritz," Lydia shouted to him. "I'm not normally the sort of girl to answer the door like that, but I figured you might have noticed on your way up."

Ben found a seat in what appeared to double up as her living room and kitchen. It was not as easy as Lydia had made it seem with her instructions. Every surface in the apartment seemed covered in the consequences of one of two things: the regular-life messes, like dirty dishes and unsorted laundry; and the New Year's party messes, like beer cans, and spillages, crumbs from chips and confetti from party poppers, playing cards and poker chips, and the unmistakable scent of day-old Chinese takeaway. He had to sweep some of the New Year's mess to one side, while trying not to sit upon a pile of clothes, but eventually he managed to sit.

It did nothing for his confidence when Lydia reappeared, though the addition of pants helped detract his attention from how she looked, to some extent. She handed him a glass of water, which he gratefully hid behind until he could find the words to speak to her.

"We don't get many door-to-door salesmen around here, you know. Especially not ones who come empty-handed." She sat in a chair full of clothes, sinking into the pile as if it were her throne, and she were its queen. "So, what did you wake me up for?"

He looked away shyly, taking a sip from the glass. The water was ice cold, and he became aware of a chill in the air. His eyes landed on her bed, visible from his seat through the door she'd gone through; aside from being a bit crumpled on top, it didn't look like it had been slept in. The Scythe whined in his head, and his attention was turned to the table, and the Chinese food. The box it had come in was still full.

"Something's wrong," he muttered.

"You want to say that louder?"

"This place is freezing, but you were just walking around like it was nothing. And your bed doesn't look like you've actually slept in it. And... you didn't eat your takeaway. You live alone here, right?" She nodded, her mouth twisted into a grimace. "What's wrong with you, Lydia?"

"How do you know my name?" she snapped.

"I have a list," he told her. It didn't feel like a lie, but it didn't make him feel better to tell her. "What's your story?"

She stood up, but she kept her distance from him. She busied herself grabbing cans and empty plates from the table. "I had a party," she told him. "You know, the usual. Invite everyone over because you have *some* space, get too drunk, and forget half the night. It was New Year's. That's the way it's supposed to happen."

He stayed put while she hid herself away in the kitchen area. He'd had nights like that, waking up on the floor of the kitchen next to Macy without a clue how he'd gotten there. But there was something different about Lydia's version, something that she wasn't saying. He wanted to press her on it, but when he thought about everything he had seen so far, he wasn't so sure questions were the solution to every problem. He waited, while she composed herself.

It took her a couple of minutes before she turned around. He thought she might have been crying, but her eyes were clear. "Have you ever been depressed?" she asked him outright. "My mom was, when she gave birth to my little brother. Post-natal craziness, or whatever. She didn't sleep much. She barely ate. That's what it feels like, except..." She huffed, grabbing shirts and folding them to distract herself from the conversation.

"Except? Keep talking," Ben told her.

She shook her head. "I don't know why I'm telling you this. Just tell me what you're selling, finish your water, then get out. I'm not feeling the whole 'polite' thing, anymore."

Standing up, he willed the Scythe out of hiding. It appeared in his hand as if had always been there, blade glowing blood red. "I'm not selling anything," he told her. "I've come to ask you to let go of life. It's necessary."

Ben had a few expectations about how people would react to a statement like that. The first was Martha Underwood's: complete soul corruption, burn everything in sight, and refuse to listen. The second was closer to Arnold Schultz's response: willingly give in to the circumstances, especially if the occasion had been planned weeks, months or even years in advance. He did not expect, in his limited experience so far, that someone would react how Lydia May did, by dumping the clothes in her hands, marching up to him, and punching him right in the nose.

He had been punched before. School hadn't been the toughest of affairs for him. He'd been in a couple of fights, and lost, but by and large the bullies had avoided him. Ben thought he was weird now, but back in school he was, by his reckoning, the single most ordinary person in the yearbook. His short history of after-school violence had prepared him for a moment like this. He knew it would hurt for a few minutes. If he was lucky, nothing would be broken. If his nose bled, he had to let it.

Aside from the pain, nothing else about the way Lydia punched him was like anything he'd felt before. That is to say, her punch was exactly like every other decent punch he had ever been on the receiving end of, but his face didn't behave as he thought it might. He stumbled backwards out of shock, but was otherwise okay. No broken nose, no blood, no lasting consequences.

"What was that for?" he asked her when he was sure he was alright.

"You pulled out... that. Whatever that is," she shouted, gesturing wildly to the Scythe. "What's with the cosplay prop?"

He sighed, and rubbed his nose again to make sure it definitely wasn't bleeding. "This might be hard for you to understand. I don't know. It was weird for me, and that was just yesterday, so maybe I'm still figuring it out." She glared at him, the same sort of look Jean would often shoot his way when she was annoyed at him. He was already beginning to associate that look on Lydia's face with her fists. "I'm… Death?"

Ben's only experience with this statement came from Gary's introduction; it had not been an easy truth to digest.

Lydia seemed less fazed by it. "Oh," she said. She sat down on the pile of clothes again. "Is that, like, your name?"

"No, my name is Ben. Ben Cooper. Death is more like my day job. I think. I'm pretty new to this." His smile came off weak, no matter how much he forced it. "The short version of how this is supposed to go is that I'm supposed to get in, convince you to pass quietly, and take your soul with the Scythe if you don't or can't. It's not fun, and it's not my choice. I wasn't lying when I said I had a list."

She nodded, pinching her arm. "Well, I'm not dreaming. But I'm not sick." She said it so confidently that Ben believed her, but it didn't explain why he was here. "So, unless you're saying I'm about to be in some terrible accident, I think you've made a mistake."

"This doesn't make sense." Ben pulled out the file. He tried not to think about where it came from or where it went. When Lydia stood up to get a better look at what he was holding, the Scythe glowed brighter, an obvious warning that convinced her to sink back into the armchair. "There's no cause of death," he told her. "It just says that you're dying. Like, right now, you're dying." The Scythe sang a tune at the back of his head. "Yeah… in a soul corruption sort of way."

"Soul corruption?" she scoffed.

"It's a whole thing. Trust me."

"Trust the guy in the sweater with the giant ass blade standing in my living room? Right."

She was eyeing the Scythe in annoyance. Every bit of her seemed human. Martha Underwood may not have punched him in the nose, but Ben was noticing a few differences between her and Lydia. Lydia was more in control of herself, sceptical of Ben's admissions rather than violently attempting to thwart him.

The file couldn't be wrong. The Scythe was attempting to reassure him of that, in its own way. "I don't like this," he said to it, ignoring the look from Lydia. "It's time to do your thing." He turned his attention back to her. "It's painless, and it's necessary. You won't like what would happen if I just left you the way you are."

"Well maybe I don't want a guy I just met attacking me," she replied. But she didn't move. She sat there, staring at the Scythe, awash in the glow of the blade as it drew closer to her. Ben eased it against her bare skin, and while she winced at what Ben assumed to be the cold of the metal, that was it. He pulled the Scythe back. "Was that it? Am I dead, now?"

The Scythe screamed in Ben's head.

"Something's wrong," Ben muttered. "Calm down," he told the Scythe, and it quietened down. "Slow down, and try your best to tell me what's wrong. Why couldn't you do it?"

Lydia laughed from across the room. "Is your little stick having performance issues?"

Ben frowned as the Scythe responded. "I don't understand," Ben moaned. "What's wrong with her soul that you can't take it out?"

The music from the Scythe blared in his head again. He let go of the handle, and it zipped out of sight. He clamped both hands over his ears, trying to block out any other noises. Lydia was speaking, but he couldn't make out any words coming from her mouth. He thought he might pass out from the pain that welled in his head.

"Calm down," Ben shouted.

The tone changed, but the volume remained high as the Scythe did its best to communicate with its new partner. He thought about Gary. He wished his supervisor could be with him, to help explain what was going on, to help interpret the song of the Scythe.

"Please just calm down," Ben whispered. "Tell me what's wrong."

Gone.

The word ripped through his head, silencing the music in an instant. Ben removed his hands from his ears, and the sounds of the Bronx rushed back. He stared at Lydia, and figured she must have realised something was happening.

Ben covered his mouth. "Gone?" he whispered. The Scythe sang back a response with a single beat. He frowned, but he at least understood what that one meant, even if it wasn't the verbal message he was looking for.

"What is it?" Lydia asked him. "What's going on?"

He pulled out her file again, shaking his head. She was no longer dying. As far as the file was concerned, as far as HQ was concerned, Lydia May was dead. But he and the Scythe knew, there was more to this than the words on the page.

"I don't know how to explain this. I need to figure this out. God…" She looked at him with pleading eyes, and he closed his eyes. "Your soul is gone, Lydia. The whole reason I'm here, and it was for nothing."

She shook her head, and it seemed like that was all she could do. He didn't think she understood the significance of what he had just said – he wasn't so sure he really understood everything that was happening in his life, either – but she seemed to accept that it wasn't a throwaway comment on Ben's part.

"Is that why I am the way I am?" she asked. "Is there something you can do about it?"

"I can try," he told her. "I promise I'll try. I'm sure my supervisor can figure something out. I'm sure the Scythe knows someone who can help."

That was the last thing Ben had the chance to say to Lydia on his first visit to her apartment. Upon mention of it, the Scythe took matters into its own hands. There was no more time for words, when words were so rarely understood by the Reapers. There was no more need for conversation with the undying girl of the Bronx, when she knew as much about the supernatural as Ben had when he had met Gary.

Without asking, and without feeling a need to, the Scythe pulled him out of Lydia May's apartment. They had answers to find.

Paul Carroll

Chapter Six: Domus Mortis

A Reaper's Scythe is his or her most valuable tool. Having come into existence long before the Reaper, and containing as much of a semblance of sentience as can be imbued in an otherwise inanimate object, a Scythe is a source of immense power and knowledge. The list of things that a Scythe is aware of that its Reaper may not be is often a lot longer than any Reaper would care to admit. This list often includes any immediate danger to the Reaper – without whom, a Scythe is useless – and any necessary locations that a Reaper might need to visit.

Unfortunately for Benjamin Cooper, there was something his Scythe did not know when it pulled him from the apartment of Lydia May in the Bronx to a quiet neighbourhood outside of Boston. That something proved rather unsettling for the young Reaper, who found himself soaring through the air after a somewhat painful landing against an invisible wall.

He landed in an awkward heap across the road from a quaint house, fitted with white picket fence and the American Dream in abundance. The Scythe, doing its job to some extent, prevented Ben from suffering any serious injuries, aside from those to his pride and clothing.

"Next time, you warn me when you're going to do that," he told it.

He expected a loud, inaudible response from the Scythe. Instead, it hid itself. Ben couldn't imagine why. The house across the street – the house he imagined the Scythe had been trying to land beside – looked as ordinary as one might imagine a house *could* look. It had an ordinary mailbox, an ordinary tree in the front garden with an ordinary tyre swing, and an ordinary black door with a golden knocker. It had a perfect white picket fence, and the grass was freshly mown.

Everything about the house was ordinary, and unmoving.

The Scythe finally chirped in his head, and though it was a wordless sound, Ben was sure they were on the same page. "If I was trying to hide, and I knew people were looking for something weird, I'd try to make myself look as ordinary as possible," he said to himself. It was how people survived high school. It was how most people kept their jobs, despite any unusual habits or interests they might have in their spare time.

Ben crossed the street, and became aware of a barrier up against the fence. He opened the gate and stepping through effortlessly. He was greeted with silence from the Scythe, no matter how hard he listened out for it. Frowning, he progressed towards the house. Something bothered him about the garden; up close, the tyre swing looked like it had never been used. The grass looked like it had never been cut – or had ever even needed to be cut.

He tapped his knuckles against the door, rather than touching the knocker. It opened quickly, and a familiar face looked back at him. Wearing the body of Mattie Brown, the necromancer Arnold Schultz let out a loud laugh. "Well shit, kid, I didn't think I'd be seeing you this soon." He stood back and ushered Ben into the house.

The house seemed to stretch on forever once the door was closed. To the left when he came in, Ben could see inside a library that towered taller than the house had been from the outside. It was something out of a fairy tale, dark wooden shelves holding up thousands of leather-bound volumes. Candles drifted between the shelves, floating along little saucers in mid-air.

Ben wanted to have a look inside, but Arnold reached across the threshold and pulled the door closed. "Sorry. Maybe when I can trust you a little bit better, and when you're not such a novice to this world." He led Ben through into a living room. It wasn't at all what Ben expected from a necromancer.

Brightly lit, with a few white chairs facing a coffee table, everything in the room seemed to have its place. There were large books on the table, which Ben was disappointed to see were the sort of titles he could pick up in his local bookstore. One wall was entirely lined with books, all commercial titles ranging from crime fiction to business books, with a few frames dotted along the wall. Ben couldn't get close enough to make out the faces in any of the pictures, but inside he laughed at the idea that none of the photographs were of Arnold, anymore.

Opposite the books were shelves filled with what Ben could only describe as magical miscellanea – or, if he were to guess, what people expected them to look like. He wasn't sure Arnold was the sort of person to leave things like that out in the open, not when he kept his books on the supernatural world in an entirely separate room. Ben was sure that the small cauldron beside the pestle and mortar was only there for show, that the dreamcatcher was merely decorative, that the silver dagger was less threatening to werewolves than folklore suggested, and that the broom hanging over the mantle was not, in fact, capable of flight.

"When you're done admiring the décor, I'll get the kettle boiling," Arnold said to him with a smirk. He strolled through the house. Mattie Brown's body seemed to be doing the necromancer well, Ben thought. He certainly seemed a happier man than the one the Scythe had shown him at the bank.

Arnold's kitchen was like his living room. That is to say, it was not at all what Ben expected. The boiling kettle ran on electricity. The worktops were made from granite, glistening from having been cleaned, with clean white mugs laid out. Arnold directed Ben into a seat at a large, round table.

"When I get house calls, I like to make sure things look right," Arnold explained. "People want to see weird magical stuff on display, even if only a tenth of it actually does anything, but they also want hot water from a kettle they can buy themselves. Tea or coffee? You look like a tea kind of person." He didn't wait for a response. "Anyone is welcome at my door," he continued. "Vampires can't get in without an invitation, magicians tend to know better than to come here, normal humans just want to pay me for my services, and Reapers... well, despite what you may have heard about necromancers, death is not welcome inside this house."

Ben had heard nothing about necromancers that hadn't come directly from Arnold's own mouth, but he didn't think it was worth bringing that up. "So, my Scythe?" he asked.

"It's here, but it isn't," Arnold replied. "Sort of like the whole supernatural world to regular humans. Technically, that Scythe is where it always goes whenever you're not holding it, but within this house, it can't be used. Maybe I'm a little bit paranoid."

"Or maybe you don't want more Reapers coming after you," Ben added. "The Scythe showed me some stuff about you. You hurt them." Arnold seemed unfazed by the accusation. "I guess you had your reasons. Like them wanting to kill you."

The necromancer laughed. "I like you, kid. You understand people better than most Reapers." He placed a cup of tea in front of Ben, and sat opposite him. "Now, let's get down to business. What are you here for?"

"I can't afford to pay you," Ben told him. "The Scythe brought me here."

Arnold shrugged. "I wasn't immediately chased down after taking this body, so I imagine you didn't tell them the exact details of the deal I had with your Scythe's former owner. You kept my secret, and that's keeping me safe from your kind. And your kind are a little bit obnoxious about killing me, if I'm being honest, so I figure a little bit of help is the least I can do. It'll help me pass the time." He took a sip from his cup. "Damn. Mattie's not a coffee drinker." He pushed the cup away from himself looking disappointed for the first time since Ben met him.

"Well, okay…" he said. "There's a girl. The file says she's dead, but she's not. I was talking to her when she should have died, and I was still talking to her before I came here." Arnold nodded, eyeing his own cup suspiciously. "And the Scythe said she doesn't have a soul."

The necromancer looked up. "That's a new one," he said with a grin.

"Is it possible?" Ben asked. "Is it possible for someone to not have a soul? Because she was pretty not dead last time I saw her."

Arnold nodded. "There's a few cases of people talking around without souls. Vampires don't have them, but that's more of a safe-keeping situation on their part. They live a long time, but that usually doesn't do well for a soul unless they know how to take care of it, like yours truly. I'm going to guess this girl wasn't a vampire, or you wouldn't have been sent to see her."

"A botch job at necromancy can also leave a soul without a body. It's where zombie myths come from. We're talking *Dawn of the Dead*, not *The Walking Dead*. If a body is revived but its soul isn't put back into it, it causes complications. Usually some irritability. Often some murder. A soul binds someone to their humanity, and necromancy is a dark art. Play with one and not the other, and you're asking for trouble."

"And that's it?" Ben asked. "She didn't look like she'd died. The Scythe didn't think she'd died."

"Someone would know if necromancy was used," Arnold explained. "Only other case of a no-soul walking around is a curious little Londoner, name of Kurt Crane. I can't figure out if I trust the guy or not, but he's definitely beyond my help if he ever needs it." He got up and poured his coffee down the sink. "There's an awful lot to this. I'm not sure you're ready."

Ben wished he could brandish the Scythe to emphasise how ready he was, but simply told Arnold, "It's my job. I don't have a choice."

The necromancer smiled, and nodded. "Okay. Crash course. To a lot of people, this is theory. To me, it's practice. It's my job. Souls are fragile and breakable. They need a nice little meat suit to keep them safe. A necromancer can bring a soul back from Beyond, but they also need to put it in a body. Thing is, if it's done right, any body will do. Bodies are just currency. If you can collect enough of the sense of self of the person from the soul, any old meat suit will do. In my case, there was a bit of a mind-switch required, too." He leaned in close. "Little secret from me to you? The soul is where the magic is kept. If, for some reason, I forgot to transfer both my mind *and* my soul into dear old Mattie here, *he* would have my power. This girl of yours, if she really has no soul, she's not safe. Not to other people, and not to herself. The soul directs the body in ways you can't imagine."

Ben thought of Lydia, of her apartment and the look in her eyes. "She's not eating. Or sleeping. She should have been freezing, but she wasn't."

"I need to see this for myself," Arnold told him. "I've got a little trick. You probably won't like it."

"Will it help Lydia?" Ben asked.

Arnold shrugged. "It might. It'll help me understand her better."

"Then do it."

He had Ben stand up. Face to face, Arnold placed his hands on either side of Ben's head. He almost looked ready to laugh. "Well, you asked for this. *Areshay ymay ivinglay emoriesmay ofway ethay undyingway irlgay.*" The moment he finished speaking, Arnold planted his lips against Ben's. A spark of magic passed through them; the moment their lips separated, Ben found his mouth moving of its own accord, words spilling out of him uncontrollably.

Through a fog, Ben could see Lydia again, exactly as he had seen her before. The minutes he had spent with her played out in order, as if on fast forward, but this time he didn't feel as if he were alone with her. He was keenly aware that Arnold's hands still held onto him, holding him in place while he exchanged words with Lydia.

He took a gasp, and Arnold let go of him. Ben fell into his chair, and Arnold frowned. "I told you that you wouldn't like it," Arnold remarked. The room was spinning, the necromancer's words dancing around Ben's head. "Have a drink. It'll help, I promise."

Ben did as instructed, and everything settled at once. "What was that?" he asked.

"Living memories," Arnold told him. "I needed to see what you saw, and you had to let me. Even if you didn't realise you were doing it." He took his own seat again. "I hate to tell you this, but your Scythe was right. She doesn't have a soul. But it's more than that. There's something seriously wrong with her."

"Is it the sort of wrong you can fix?"

Arnold shook his head. "This isn't necromancy. It's something else. But maybe I can still help. It'll give me something interesting to do while I figure out how Mattie's body works." He shot Ben a grin once more.

"You're sure you want to do this for free?"

"Consider it a favour to the new guy. Something like this coming along on your second day? You need all the help you can get."

It was not the vote of confidence that Ben was looking for, but it would do. Maybe, he thought, it would be enough to save Lydia May.

Chapter Seven: Damage Control

Ben was not used to the sound of his own phone, but for the second time that morning it rang from an unknown number. Arnold ignored Ben as he answered it, lost in his own thoughts about Lydia.

"Mister Cooper," a voice said to him. "I'm calling from Damage Control."

"Damage Control?"

Arnold's attention snapped back to the room. "Don't mention me," he whispered. "They don't like me. You're not here."

"We need you to come in, Mister Cooper," the woman on the other end of the line told him.

Ben couldn't help but wonder if she was human. He knew better than to ask. "It's Ben. What's this about?"

"Just a formality. We'll be expecting you." With that, she had hung up, and Arnold was eyeing him up with suspicion.

Ben pocketed his phone. "Who are Damage Control, and why does no one I'm supposed to work with know proper phone etiquette?" he asked Arnold.

The necromancer shrugged. "Phones are boring, I guess. Most of these people don't live in the real world. They're completely obsessed with the supernatural that they forget other people aren't. They don't bother with social decorum." He let out a laugh. "Man, Damage Control. That brings me back. Those guys hate me."

"But who are they?"

"Just, you know… the clean-up crew. I kept them busy for a few decades during my wild youth. Those were the days." He began counting on his fingers. "Eleven. That's how many of them have sworn mortal vengeance on me for the amount of trouble I caused them. Half of them died. The Reapers in those days almost left their souls on Earth, hoping I'd run into them and get stuck in a fight I couldn't win." He stood up from the table, and began leading Ben towards the front door. "You should really get going. They're not incredibly patient, and I have to head into my library. You know, your no-go zone. Someone's got to figure out what's up with our undying friend in the Bronx."

Arnold pushed him into the garden and slammed the door shut behind him. Something about the way the necromancer was unfailingly brutal in his honesty was refreshing against the backdrop of Gary's easing-in education into the world of the supernatural. He was smiling as he left the garden, a tingle running down his back as he passed through Arnold's barrier.

In an instant, the Scythe pulled him away from the house, dropping him just inside the front door of Damage Control. "You can't keep doing that," he snapped at the Scythe, urging his stomach to settle down.

He ignored its response, his eyes falling on the oversized badge of Damage Control behind the front desk. Rounded off by angel wings, the badge showed a sword, staff and sceptre in a triangle, a fire at their centre. Around the edges of the crest, Ben read the words *Dum vita est, spes est*. Every bit of it went over his head, and straight to his heart. The Scythe was quiet and reserved as he stood there, the weight of the crest settling on him.

"Can I help you?" a man asked. He wore a plain black uniform, the shirt-tie-and-pants combination of law enforcement, with a brass badge attached to his chest.

Ben nodded. "I got a call saying I had to come in. Benjamin Cooper?"

The man pulled out his phone, searching through a list of names with quick flicks of his finger. "The new Reaper?" Ben nodded. "Take the elevator down three floors. There's someone waiting there for you. Unless you need something else?"

"Well, maybe some idea about why I'm here?"

"Of course. It's standard procedure for the particular case being dealt with, to bring in an available Reaper to sign off on – well, you'll see. They probably want to get you used to it as soon as possible. Mister Murphy used to do it all the time, as the North American representative."

"So, I'm not in trouble?"

The man smiled. "I doubt it. Second day on the job, there's not much you can do wrong." He turned to return to his desk, and paused. "If you need anything, feel free to call us. Ask for Ramirez. I'll be happy to help. I remember what it's like coming into all of this for the first time."

Ramirez left before Ben could thank him properly. Having someone to talk to in the building gave him cause to relax. The way Arnold had talked about Damage Control, Ben wasn't entirely sure what to expect. Gary hadn't given him any warning about them. Becky hadn't told him he'd ever have to deal with them.

He entered the elevator and pressed the button marked B3. The air turned heavy the moment he passed beneath the surface. The Scythe complained at the sudden change. "What is this place?" he asked it, though he wasn't sure he would ever get a full answer from the blade.

The doors pinged open to an industrial steel room, rusty red and choking with heat.

"Ben," a woman called. She waved her hand, gesturing him over, and he saw no other option. Ramirez had said someone would be waiting for him. "Apologies about calling you in here like that. HQ refused to send Murphy. Change of duties, or some excuse like that. My name is Suzie Bonham. While you're below the surface, I'm the only person you should talk to. Do you understand that?"

"Yes Ma'am," Ben replied. She wasn't dressed in uniform, like Ramirez had been. She looked more civilian, dressed smartly. Her badge was identical to his, pinned to her suit jacket. While Ramirez had been a soldier standing to attention, Suzie stood with an attitude to her, the same way Arnold walked.

"You're never to call me that again," she warned him. She was younger than his mother, as far as he could tell, but infinitely fiercer. "You can call me Detective Bonham, Bonham, or Suzie. None of this 'Ma'am' crap. You'll make me feel old." She led him away from the elevators, and the walls turned from steel to stone. Ben coughed through the air, pausing in a vain attempt to catch his breath. "This place does that sometimes," she told him. "Take your time to become acclimatised. Reapers always struggle on their first visit, but it happens to others, too, magical or otherwise."

"While you're getting used to this place, I'll give you the tour. If I'm walking too fast, then you need to stop. I won't know otherwise, got it?" Ben nodded, wheezing in a burning lungful. "Upstairs is the political and marketing section of Damage Control. Folks up there, they deal with Public Relations, particularly in the event of a catastrophe – however big or small. They monitor the *Black Pages* for new additions. You know what that is, right?" Ben shook his head. "Well, you'll learn."

"Down here, we deal in the magical work of keeping things a secret. That's why the air's so hard to breathe, especially for you. There's power down here, the sort they don't like talking about outside these horrible walls. These are the original grounds for the organisation we spawned from. They're charged to keep the world safe from every danger imaginable, be it demonic, angelic, magical, or some hybrid of the three. People got real good at killing each other over the years, but there's always something else out there that needs dealing with."

She stopped outside a large, metal door. "Sometimes we're soldiers, other times we're prison guards. Most of the time, we're just the clean-up crew, fixing things when someone goes rogue. I'd show you the Damage Control 101 tape, but nothing like that works down here, and it's a little bit boring."

Finally, Ben didn't feel like he was dying. "Ramirez, the guy upstairs, he said you needed me to do something?"

Suzie smiled, as if forgetting herself. "He's a good kid. He'll go far in this business." She opened the door slowly. "In here, you're going to see something you probably wish you hadn't. As a Reaper, you're going to get a lot of that. I'm not going to make life any easier for you."

Ben had never smelled rotting flesh. He wished he'd never have to again, but something told him that wish would never come true. Suzie let him ease his way inside. There were two other people in the room, who remained quiet behind sanitary masks. They stood away from a metal table in the middle of the room.

It was definitely human, definitely in the past tense. What was left was barely recognisable. The flesh had turned purple, and was melting from the bone, oozing slowly towards the edges of the table. The hair had all but fallen out. Part of the skull was visible where the flesh had fallen away. Ben stepped in closer, morbid curiosity guiding his feet more than anything else. The organs were indistinguishable from one another, a bubbling mess in the abdomen the only remains of what had been a full digestive system.

"What happened to him?" Ben asked.

"You're sure it's a male?" Suzie asked.

He nodded. "I studied anatomy in college as part of art history. The size of the bones, the height of the body, the shape of him – one hundred percent, a man. Young?"

"Twenty-six," Suzie told him. "We have our guesses about what happened. Normally, a body like this, we'd suspect a necromancer who's up to no good, but we've heard nothing from the folks upstairs who do the necessary work of liaising with your employers."

"Could a necromancer do this?" he asked. He thought about Arnold. He didn't think he was responsible, but he might know who was.

Suzie seemed less certain, turning her attention to the men in the room with them. "What did you find out?" she asked them.

One of them, an older man, cleared his throat. "The rate of decay wasn't natural. When they found him, he looked perfectly healthy. Well, all things considered." He looked at Ben. "The man died in a car accident yesterday morning. The police reported drink driving. We got a tip that it was something else, something more deliberate."

The Scythe chimed in Ben's head, a questioning noise that rang repeatedly. He figured it wouldn't stop until he answered, but he wasn't sure how the others would react to him talking to himself. He closed his eyes, listening to the noise and attempting to think his response back to the Scythe.

When he reopened his eyes, the world had turned red. The Scythe chimed again. *See.* The word echoed in his mind, and he looked down at the man. His face, pre-melted, hovered over the body. He was barely older than Ben. A sports player, Ben though, judging by the image of the body that was spreading out in front of him. The chest looked burned, and Ben leaned in to get a closer look.

The Scythe sang another song in his head, loud and pounding and familiar.

"Gone," Ben said to himself. He stood upright, the room spinning, and normal colour returned to his eyes. Suzie looked at him quizzically. "I think I know what made him do it," he told her.

"You want to fill the rest of us in?" she asked.

"His soul." He pointed to the chest, though there was nothing left of it but bone and mush. "I bet if you have pictures of him before he looked like this, you'll see a burn on his chest. It's where his soul was removed."

Suzie nodded. "I assume you two took preliminary photos before he began to decompose like this. Find them, and verifying the facts. In the meantime, I have some paperwork for you to fill out, Ben. Standard procedure for what I've got to do next."

"Sure, but, what is it?"

She pointed to the table. "We found him yesterday morning. An hour ago, we got a call about three more, all men in their twenties. Whatever happened to our new favourite autopsy, it's not an isolated case. I need you to sign off on the removal of their bodies from the areas they were found. Anything dealing with the magic of death and the soul, that's your department."

She handed over the forms in a separate room – her office, she told him - pointing out key details where she thought they might interest him. There was no natural light in her office. No window. No ventilation. Just a desk, completely bare.

"I'm sure Officer Ramirez has already offered his assistance to you," Suzie said to him, "But don't think you've only got one ally in this building. You find out anything about this case, you tell me. I don't want any nasty surprises in the future, and I figure you don't either." He tried to force a smile. His mother often told him growing up that if he didn't know how to respond, a smile was usually a good place to start. "I know you're only new to this, Ben, but I've got bad news for you. Your job may have just gotten a whole lot more complicated."

She led him back to the elevator, where the temperature skyrocketed again. He wanted to know why, but he didn't want to ask. Something told him he wouldn't get a satisfactory answer. Between Gary and Arnold, he got the impression that people in the supernatural business liked to keep a few secrets.

"If any more bodies pop up, you'll tell me, right?"

Suzie shrugged. "If I deem it appropriate to tell you, yes. Some things aren't right for young minds, Ben." She placed a hand on his shoulder, keeping his attention until the elevator arrived. "Your line of work is going to be hard. I know from experience. Make sure you find someone to talk to, okay? Before the weight of all of this creeps up on you, if you can."

He nodded, stepping back into the elevator, praying for release for the heat. He was barely out the door when his phone buzzed in his pocket with two missed calls. It rang again before he could figure out who was calling him. "Hello?"

"Mister Cooper, it's Rena from HQ. We met this morning."

"Fangirl, right?"

She giggled for a moment down the phone. "That's me. Look, we've got a case here that we need you to look in to. Do you think you could–" Before she could finish her sentence, Ben fell onto the floor of the lobby. "Oh, hi. Nice entrance." She held a folder down over her desk for him. He took it in his hand, using it to hide his face as he climbed to his feet. If he could kill his Scythe, Ben was sure he would be trying by the end of the day.

Chapter Eight: Consecrated Weapons

Since the beginning, Reapers had a special bond with the Scythes. They were chosen for their potential in several fields: athleticism in battle, wit in war, and loyalty in their comrades. Together with their Scythes, the original Reapers protected the natural world from the corruption that came when a soul refused to pass to the Beyond. They acted as one, the Scythe the natural extension of the Reaper's will, and the Reaper the moving body of the Scythe.

Ben was told this story three times by Rena before she agreed to check if there was something wrong with the Scythe, no matter what the stories said about typically good Reapers. Her desk companion looked bored of her responses. Ben couldn't tell if that was just his resting face.

The file he had received from Rena was unlike the others. Aside from the fact that it was thicker, it was bound in black, rather than cream. Something about it made him uneasy. Rena told him in a throwaway manner that black meant it was important. That, maybe, he should know that by now, and he thought that maybe he had done something to insult her. He had bigger concerns, opening the file:

Assigned Reaper: Unresponsive.
Soul: Carlson Grimes. Misplaced.
Cause of death: stabbing.
Note: Scythe missing.

He re-read those words over and over before he could bring himself to move on. He didn't know the other

Reapers. There was no orientation process, where they all got together for team-building exercises and an ice-breaker session. One of them becoming unresponsive wasn't an immediate red flag, as far as Ben was concerned. Maybe, like Gary, they'd had enough of the job.

It was the missing Scythe that turned his stomach. The perpetual singing of his Scythe at the back of his mind, however irritable, was an indication of his position. He looked up to Rena. "Do you guys know where every Reaper is?"

She rolled her eyes. "Not exactly. We can track the Scythes, because of the energy they give off. Know where the Scythe is, and you know where the Reaper is. But we don't really check unless we can't get in touch with you for a while."

Ben looked at the date on the file. Carlson Grimes died on December 31st. "How long is a while?"

"They really didn't tell you any of this stuff? It's a twenty-four-hour thing. We take missing persons a bit more seriously than the cops, especially when it's a Reaper." She returned her attention to her work, though Ben couldn't imagine what she could be doing, given the near-comatose state of her colleague beside her.

Twenty-four hours without a response from the Reaper, and no sign of his Scythe. He looked back to the file, where a line was marked URGENT.

Displaced soul at risk of corruption if connected to missing Scythe. Proceed with caution.

Ben frowned. Another case like Mrs Underwood. He looked at the address in the file. Grimes had died in New York, but his soul was reported as being in Chicago. There was a chance that the file was wrong, Ben thought. It wouldn't be the weirdest thing to have happened to him since Gary arrived at his house.

"Okay," he said to the Scythe. "Take us there."

He almost landed perfectly in Chicago, having to catch himself before toppling over onto his face. It was better than what he was used to. He only wished that the Scythe would be more careful about where it brought them. Standing in the middle of the road, Ben was sure he was about to cause an accident.

But things were quiet in Chicago that morning. Ben looked down the street in each direction; lots of traffic, none of it turning in his direction. There were a few people walking along the sidewalk, wearing a look of regret upon their faces. The neighbourhood looked clean, safe even.

There was a single café open on the street, and only one person sitting in it. The Scythe kept itself hidden from view, but it sang within his head the same tune from his visit to Damage Control, turning the world red through his eyes. Ben walked closer to the man, glad to be out of the street. He was pale and sweating, his hands shaking with every attempt to lift his cup of coffee to his mouth.

All around him, the air was turning black. His chest was burning up, a twisted mess of multi-coloured light fighting to escape. Ben thought back to Martha Underwood's soul when he finally managed to remove it, a thread of red light weaving through the blue. Ben was far from an expert on matters to do with the soul, but by his reckoning this looked worse.

The thing that bothered him more was that the photo of the man in the file didn't match the man that he was looking at now. He wondered if the file had been wrong about the location, but the Scythe sang a different tune. As wrong as it felt to stand there in front of him, this was the man that Ben had been sent to deal with.

"Carlson Grimes?" he asked.

The man looked up, his eyes bloodshot and weary. He stared at Ben in silence for a couple of minutes; the young Reaper wasn't sure why he was humouring the stranger, but the warning in the file was keeping him at bay for the time being. If he was lucky, the corruption of his soul wouldn't manifest in quite the same way as in the Underwood case. He wasn't sure he knew what to do without Gary there to help him.

Finally, Grimes looked away. He pushed his chair back a few inches, screeching the legs against the floor as he did so. Before Ben could begin to feel sorry for him, he screamed.

The window of the café exploded outwardly at the noise from Grimes' mouth. Ben wished that had been the worst of it. Mid-scream, the table parted down the middle, sliced in two by a violet Scythe that materialised out of nothingness. The Scythe howled at Ben incomprehensibly, and his own Scythe responded, flaring into sight.

"Another one?" Grimes snarled. When he spoke, two voices layered on top of each other, one completely devoid of emotion. "I won't let you take me. I'm not ready to die." Ben thought he looked ready to cry, but instead of water from his eyes, his face began to crack and ooze purple goo.

"You're sick," Ben told him. "Whatever you're doing, wherever you got that Scythe, it's hurting you. And I don't mean the physical you. I mean your soul. Your body, it's just a… it's just a meat sack."

Grimes laughed, spitting out a couple of teeth as he did. "They're all just meat sacks. That doesn't mean I'm ready to let this one go." He raised a hand, and Ben soared backwards out of the building. Glass ripped into his clothes, but he felt it break against his skin. One perk of the Scythe, he knew, that he couldn't live without.

He stumbled to his feet, his back sore from the landing. Grimes stepped out of the café through the window, crunching glass under his feet. His face twisted into a grimace, and he swung his empty hand forward; glass from the window rose into the air, and shot towards Ben like rockets. His Scythe teleported him to the side, where he fell to his knees.

The violet Scythe came down upon him, stabbing into the ground just inches from his feet. He knew what would happen if Grimes landed a hit. He had less of an idea about how he could do the things he was doing. Another swing of the violet Scythe stole his attention. Once more he was teleported out of danger, but he knew he couldn't keep that up if his own Scythe was simply trying to avoid capture.

"We need to fight," he told it. "We don't stand a chance if we just run."

It sang loudly in his head. He didn't have time to try figure out what it wanted, raising it up in defence against a third swing of Grimes' Scythe. The weapons screamed against each other. Ben was used to the noise, but Grimes roared at it. With a swing of his arm, he threw Ben backwards into the air.

Poltergeist, the Scythe said to him.

He thought about Martha Underwood's combustible homeware. Maybe Carlson Grimes was a little less explosive, but he was more in control of the manifestation of his corruption. Enough so that Ben crashed against the ground much more roughly than he was ready for. It wasn't the best start to a new job, he knew.

Grimes was marching closer again, his Scythe casting a purple light over the whole block. Ben could hear it complaining. Everyone around them could. The café workers were crying, and the few onlookers were huddled back in fear, covering their ears against the noise of the violet Scythe. This wasn't something for mortal ears, Ben knew. Only Reapers should hear the song of the Scythe.

Ben screamed against the pain that flared up throughout his body, running towards Grimes with his Scythe ready for a swing. The other man wasn't expecting him, barely blocking a swing from Ben. The violet light subsided, and

Grimes collapsed to the ground. Ben lowered his Scythe towards Grimes' chest.

"It's time to end this," he told him.

"Not yet," Grimes spat. His chest began to glow, right where Ben had noticed the burn on the body in Damage Control. Unlike Martha Underwood, the light that spilled from Grimes had barely a small fraction of blue within it. A multitude of reds and purples spilled out of him, soaring into the air. The violet Scythe vanished at the same time, ripped away in a cloud of black smog.

Ben lowered his Scythe. He could tell without looking that the man in front of him was just like Lydia May: his soul was missing.

"What happened?" he asked, and winced against the pain in his face, where the flesh had cracked and corroded. He shut his eyes as best as he could. "Please, help me."

Ben nodded, taking out his phone. Rena answered almost immediately. "Did you see the missing Scythe?" he asked her. "There's something wrong. You need to send someone down here." The man was struggling to breathe. Ben wasn't sure if he stood a chance at surviving this. Whatever Carlson Grimes had done to him, he didn't look to be the first one. What was it Suzie Bonham had said? Three more bodies this morning? Counting in their oozing friend from the table, and Lydia, that was at least six people affected by whatever Grimes had done.

There were many things Ben did not yet know about Reaper HQ. The most significant, to him, was where they were located. Secondary to this was how they travelled anywhere. Gary, he had supposed, could teleport as a result of years as a Reaper. But when Rena appeared behind him without a word of warning, accompanied by Becky, Suzie, and a small army of men and women in black hazmat suits, that theory went up in the air. He added it to the list of things he wasn't sure he would ever get to ask about, and probably never should.

"What happened here, Ben?" Suzie asked him.

Becky cleared her throat. "I appreciate your concern for the new Reaper, Bonham, but this is my concern. You deal with the civilians." Suzie scowled, but left to examine the young man that had once been the meat sack of Carlson Grimes. "You want to fill me on this? Rena, take notes."

He hesitated. Gary had never explained the protocol for this. He had never told him how much he should say, or to who. Ben wondered where his supervisor had gone, what was so important that he couldn't make it to the scene like this.

He gave himself a few moments, and a few deep breaths, to collect his thoughts. "I have reason to believe that this isn't an isolated case," he told Becky. "The man on the ground, I think he's connected to the bodies that Suzie – that Detective Bonham – has been building a case around. And I think it's connected to the missing Scythe from New Year's Eve." He thought about mentioning Lydia, but he wasn't sure he was ready to drag her into this. Not until Arnold could find some way to help her. "The burn mark on the victim's chest is from a corrupted soul leaving his body, and taking his soul with him."

"What would he need with another soul?" Becky asked sternly.

"I could only take a guess," Ben admitted. "Maybe, for food. Maybe to try hold himself together. A soul needs a body, and a soul that survives on Earth after the body dies begins corrupting."

"Everyone knows that," Becky reminded him. "It's our business to know such things, remember?"

"But did you know that he's using a Scythe to do it?" Ben asked her. She frowned at him, but she didn't argue. "I think he's jumping from body to body, until they break down or he finds another one that he likes better. If your missing Reaper isn't dead, I think he could confirm my story about the Scythe. I saw it. It's purple, right? The way mine is red, and the others…"

Rena stared back at him quietly. Becky shook her head. "Gary shouldn't have told you that already. There's a process." She sighed. "Okay, here's how this is going to happen. We're issuing you a uniform. We expect you to use it, at least once." With a click of her fingers, a box fell into Rena's hands. She passed it over to Ben, avoided eye contact. "You'll move on to your next case. Bonham will examine the young man over there, and deal with the public spectacle you put on here. We'll look into this…body snatcher." She turned around, ready to leave with Rena, whose excitement from the morning's arrival of Kerubiel was finally wearing off completely, before adding, "And, well done, Mister Cooper. If you're right, you did well to defend yourself. At least long enough for us to do something about it."

They disappeared in a flash of light – Ben decided it was a Headquarters thing – leaving him standing there with a box, a suddenly-appearing file, a hazmat army, and the latest victim in a case he wasn't sure he really understood.

Chapter Nine: Deathly Serious

When a Reaper wasn't wearing his or her uniform, it could easily be mistaken for a Halloween costume, waiting for the application of makeup to the wearer, and the addition of a plastic scythe. It was, to the human eye, a simple, heavy robe, black all over with a hood to keep it suitable for all weathers. The cloth was softer than expected, darker than the night sky, and a challenge to pull over one's head. Ben now understood why Gary had excused himself to the rest room when he was changing.

He struggled to remove the rest of his clothes, tucked away in the small toilet of the café in Chicago. Suzie had the staff preoccupied, leaving him the privacy to crash against the wall in a fit against the robe. Even free from the worry of being heard, he only just about managed to pull the robe over his head.

The moment he pulled the hood up, the inside of the robe turned dark; his pale skin was lost to the void of smoke and shadow that swam outwards, his feet lost where the robe brushed the floor.

While Ben's eyesight stayed clear and true, his eyes melted from their sockets. He watched them in the mirror of the rest room, red lights burning where once there had been flesh. His skin pulled taut against the bone, and slithered away, baring his teeth. His hair was hidden beneath the hood, but he could still feel the individual strands plucked away by an invisible force, individually and across his head at random. He reached up instinctively to feel it, and could only stare at the bony replacement at the end of his wrist.

"So, this is it?" he asked himself. His mouth had refused to move, but the words still bounced around inside his head. He prodded at his jaw, but his mouth remained sealed. "I guess it's part of the uniform."

The Scythe sang in his head, jumping into his skeletal hand with more vigour and energy than ever before. He supposed it was used to Reapers who fit the job description down to the letter. It looked right, a dead man holding the Scythe. It was as things were meant to be.

That didn't make it any easier to look in the mirror. He resolved to quit that practice; he wasn't sure he'd ever see himself the same way after witnessing the transformation from deer-in-headlights.

The file fell from his sleeve into his hand. He scanned it quickly, and sighed. It wasn't like anything else they'd issued him with, yet. He wondered if that were deliberate, or if he had simple been lucky with his home visits. He would have swallowed hard in anticipation of opening the door to the restroom, if he could remember how to do it.

The moment the lock opened, the Scythe teleported them away from Chicago. Even unprepared, Ben was unfazed by the action. His feet glided above the ground, landing on a black cloud. His robe stretched to the floor, pouring out darkness. He felt taller, floating above the floor as he was.

He was in a hospital. Ben was aware of a sterile smell in the air, though he wasn't sure how his missing nose was picking up anything. There were nurses rushing in every direction, doctors seeing to their patients in every room, dozens of people waiting around – either patients or their families – and not a single pair of eyes looking in his direction.

That wasn't to say no one could see him. He had practice in avoiding the gaze of someone in the street – usually someone looking to sign him up for monthly donations – and recognised that same expression upon the faces of some of those he saw before him. A few patients had become rigged with fear. A nurse behind her station glanced at him with an inhuman glimmer in her eyes, albeit briefly. A couple of visitors to the ward were trying their hardest to stay out of his way as he walked through the corridors.

He didn't know how his feet knew the way. The path merely formed in his stride, such that he no longer needed to concern himself with human decisions and the fallibility of doubt. The air was cooling rapidly around him, forcing people to wrap their coats around themselves as he passed.

The door to the room he was headed to opened itself for him as he came close, and the hospital seemed to freeze. The busyness of movement slowed to a fraction of its speed, steps pausing in mid-air, coughs catching in throats, and the beeping of the EKG silenced itself in his presence.

The room was full. A young woman sat up in her bed, her parents, friends and extended family standing around her. She looked around the room in confusion. It was as if she were sitting in a photograph. Ben strode up beside her.

"Is this real?" she asked. He nodded slowly. "Do you know who I am? Do you know what's wrong with me?"

He had memorised it from the file. "Your name is Cady Summers. You're twenty-two years old, and you've been fighting cancer since you were a teenager." She didn't look sick. She was pale, but it was winter, so that was to be expected. Her hair was short, like it had been growing back for some time. Her eyes looked tired, and her arms were thin, but he would never have guessed that it was her time to go. "Do you know who *I* am?"

She shrugged. "I didn't think you were real," she admitted.

He felt like smiling. The thing about having a naked skull for a head, of course, was that smiles were impossible. Emotional responses were verbal, and only if he could really force himself to feel something. There were no butterflies in his stomach, no pounding of his chest as he looked at this girl who should have been starting her career, the same way Jean was.

"I was like you, until yesterday," he told her. "Maybe not exactly like you, but oblivious to... this." He gestured to his uniform with his free hand. The Scythe stayed quiet. It left him to do his job. "A lot of things are real. I'm sure I can tell you that. There are a lot of things I *could* tell you. But the most important is this: death is inevitable."

Cady smiled weakly. "I know that."

"You're not afraid?"

"Of course I'm afraid," she scoffed. She looked at her parents, standing over her bed. Her mother's mouth was twisted between syllables. Her father had tears welling in his eyes that, maybe, no one was supposed to see. "They're the ones who need to be told that this can't be stopped. We've been through it all. Chemo. Radiation therapy. Rehab. Dropping out of school to be home-schooled. Thinking I was in the clear. I'm ready for this. It's the only thing I haven't tried, yet."

Ben nodded. "We don't visit just everyone, you know. We have a list. People who'd stay if we didn't interfere at some point." He sighed, a chill pushing through the room. "I haven't been doing this for very long, so I don't know how much it means to you for me to say this, but I haven't seen anything like this before. All of these people, all here for you. Maybe it's to say goodbye. Maybe it's to say that they love you. Maybe it's to make things easier for themselves in the face of what's to come. They're why I'm here."

"You're not going to do anything to them, are you?"

"Only the worst thing they can imagine," Ben replied.

She wiped her eyes before a tear could fall free. "I promised myself that I wouldn't cry about this anymore. They have me here for more tests. Another brain scan, to see if there's anything that can be done to save me. They keep clinging on to this hope that I'll be okay, but what about them? What's going to happen to them?"

"They'll break a little bit inside, and then they'll try to pull the piece back together. That's all anyone can do when they lose someone they love. And they do love you, Cady. I know that. Not because of the money they spent on medical bills. Not because they keep fighting to keep you alive. I know it because if they didn't love you so much, I wouldn't need to do my job. There wouldn't be anything holding you back from passing on quietly. That love will hurt them, but it's made them stronger. It might take a while, but they'll make it through this."

The words came from him as quickly as he could think of them. He poured as much empathy as he could muster into them, however flat they sounded out whenever he spoke. He wanted to show her tears. He wanted to show her sorrow. He wanted to do anything to make her see that even Death was sympathetic to her plight, that even Death understood that dying wasn't the most difficult thing in the world for Cady.

A tear fell from her father's eye, and Ben felt the Scythe sing. "It's time," he told her. "There will be a few moments after this for you, while your body catches up. It'll be okay."

"Do it," she told him, looking away as he moved the Scythe closer to her. He rested the tip of the blade against her chest. Slowly, blue light poured out of her, sinking into the Scythe. When the light finally faded, he took a step back. There was no burn. There was nothing to show that he had ever been there.

The room came back into motion as soon he made his exit. He tried not to look as Cady took a sharp breath. He tried not to look when her EKG levelled out. He tried not to look as her mother screamed and her father cried.

But he did.

Ben couldn't help it. He watched them attempt to resuscitate her, fighting the inevitable. Grief flooded the ward, drowning the young Reaper. He let the Scythe pull them away.

Home. It brought him back to his bedroom, the door closed, the blinds drawn, everything exactly as he had left it that morning, with the exception of a small bundle at the end of his bed – someone had brought his clothes home for him.

He thought about Cady, and inevitably thought about Martha, and Carlson, and Lydia. His undying girl, his secret from Damage Control. He recalled the way she had looked when she answered the door to him, fiery and beautiful and every bit of her trying to make his early appearance at her door a matter of business. She had been a perfect host in an imperfect apartment. She had listened when he spoke to her. And he had left her there, waiting for answers, completely unaware that there were more people like her in the world, and that almost all of them had died as a result of what they'd been through.

His heart did not beat for her. He breathed as easily as he if he were making a sandwich when he thought about what might happen to her. He looked at his reflection in the mirror, at the black robe that covered him from head to toe.

"I am become a Death," he mused, and felt none of the embarrassment or disgust at himself that he was aiming for. There was simply black smoke, and the void of darkness.

CHAPTER TEN: ONCE MORE WITH FEELING

Ben took to the bathroom to change into his own clothes again, a process which began with the removal of the uniform. Rather than simply lower the hood, he began pulling at the robe, lifting it upwards over his head and dumping it all at once onto the floor. Smoke still clung to his body, holding his underwear and shoes in place as his organs began to grow back into place.

His heartbeat filled the room, unrestrained by lungs, flesh, or skin. He took a gasp of air, two balloons filling his ribcage. A thousand knives stabbed him all over, nerves finding their way back into the world. Muscle stretched over bone, tied up in cartilage and fat, all bundled together neatly in pale skin, covering his body in one seamless motion while his digestive system took a turn for the worse.

Hot bile spewed up his re-growing oesophagus, lashing against his tongue and forcing his mouth open for the first time. He spat into the toilet, tears rolling down his eyes as they sprouted back into his head.

Ben didn't know why he cried. The pain was fine, he thought. The pain was temporary, every sensation fading back to normality after a few seconds. He could deal with his feet feeling too big in his shoes, or his hands feeling fat as he tried to hold himself over the bowl of the toilet.

Maybe it was Cady. Maybe it was that she was the same age as Jean, but didn't get to live any longer than that. Maybe it had been watching her like that, when his job was already done, when no one could save her. Maybe it was that the same thing would happen to Jean, eventually, or that it had almost been his father. Maybe-maybe-maybe. His stomach gave in again, and more bile poured from his mouth.

"How did Gary do this?" Ben mumbled to the Scythe. It was silent, but he was aware it was there, the same way he knew his hair was on his head and his hands were at the ends of his wrists. "Well, is there *anyone* to talk to about it?"

A knock on the door interrupted his train of thought. "Ben? Is that you in there?"

Jean. He pushed himself up, wiping his mouth with some tissue and flushing. "Yeah, I'll be out in a minute," he told her.

"We didn't hear you come in." Silence. There was more. There were questions. With Jean, there were always questions. How was his day? What's it like watching someone die? Is your skeleton as weird looking as you think it might be? Instead, "Come downstairs and say hi, okay?"

She didn't wait for a response. He listened to her footsteps on the stairs, the squeak of certain steps that he knew how to avoid whenever he needed to. When she was gone, really gone, he pulled on the rest of his clothes, ditching his shoes along the way. His reflection looked normal again, like nothing had ever happened. Still, he couldn't keep his eyes trained on it for very long. The glowing red eyes found a way to stare back at him, whether he wore them or not.

Ben didn't take his time walking downstairs. His parents and Jean were sitting at the dining table, Macy waiting for him by the empty chair. Hefty portions of potatoes and vegetables were steaming on his plate. Amanda looked at him expectantly. "You know, I never expect a thank you, but I do expect you to sit down with us," she told him.

"I'm not that hungry," he said.

She dropped her knife and fork. Her own dinner had barely been touched. Martin had just started. "What did you eat today?" she asked him. "What did you have for breakfast, when you left before sunrise? Where did you go for lunch?" She almost looked like she might wait for an answer, but she wouldn't have been Amanda Cooper, Overbearing Mother of the Year, 1992-2017, if she did. "What about yesterday? And don't get me started about the day before – I know *all* about that."

"Amanda," Martin whispered.

"No, Martin," she snapped. "Ben, I don't want a repeat of before. I don't want you getting sick again. Now tell me the truth."

He hesitated, which in most circumstances Amanda would have interpreted as an admission of guilt. Ben would have, too, if he didn't know better. Hunger had completely eluded him. Even looking at the dinner Amanda had put on the table, his stomach was silent and his mouth was dry.

He sat down without a word, shovelling a forkful of mash potato into his mouth. Amanda smiled, and began eating her own dinner slowly. Jean didn't let Ben slow himself down, heaping slices of roast chicken onto his plate for him, and dousing it all in gravy before returning to her own dinner.

Ben was scraping his plate clean before Martin was even half-way through.

"Better?" Amanda asked him. He nodded slowly. "A mother always knows. It's only been a couple of days, Ben. I know this is new to you. I know it's probably not easy. But you can't just run off without eating anything. There's not enough of you to do that, especially not when you could just let yourself starve for days on end if no one stopped you."

"Thanks," he whispered.

He sat with them while they ate. Jean had more questions than Ben knew the answers to, and he had fewer things he'd like to talk about than she was happy with. He told her about hospital, but he didn't mention the uniform, or give her too much information about Cady. He told her about Damage Control, but he left out anything to do with the body snatcher. He omitted the entire ordeal with Carlson Grimes, in fact, afraid that his parents would worry about him every time he stepped outside to deal with a case. He knew that for every Carlson there were a million Cadys. He knew that Martha and the body snatcher, two days in a row, were just flukes. There was no way Gary wouldn't have told him if they were the norm.

The Coopers were good at secrets, but Ben knew that there was only so long they could go before his all came out.

"Why did I need to take this job?" Ben asked them suddenly. The words came out of his mouth before he could stop them.

"It was the only way to save your father," Amanda said to him.

"No. Why did that ever happen? Jean and I deserve to know why we almost lost our dad. You owe that to us."

Martin and Amanda shared a look, waiting a few moments before he placed his cutlery out of his hands. "We always wondered if we'd have this conversation with you. Until yesterday, we weren't sure it would ever come up. It was 1991. We were a few years older than you, and we'd been married for half our relationship. Young love did that to people back then. Lock them in before they find someone more interesting."

"We wondered for a long time if it was the worst thing we could have done to each other," Amanda added. "We'd been trying for a few years, and…"

"Trying what?" Ben asked.

"To have a baby. We'd been trying to have a baby."

"But we weren't a good fit," Martin explained. "Your mother and I, we weren't able to have kids. Treatment back then, it was expensive. I was still relatively new to the firm, and your mother wasn't working at the time."

"I wanted to be an artist," she muttered.

"We couldn't adopt. Circumstances, waiting lists, timing – everything seemed stacked against us."

Amanda placed a hand on Martin's. "We begged for help, anywhere we could, until someone finally responded to our call. You know, you want something for long enough, and you ask for it hard enough, sometimes the universe listens. We got a limited time offer, a short-term fix to our problems. A couple of years to have a couple of kids, at a price."

"Most people had college debts over their heads. Ours was always a little more literal," Martin joked.

Jean looked to Ben, whose face had gone blank while he processed. "Are you okay?"

"I don't know," he muttered. "Are we real?"

"Of course you're real," Amanda cried.

"I could pinch you to prove it, if you like," Jean said to him. "It won't change your day job. It won't change what you have to do every day for... for how long?"

The Scythe whistled in his head. His constant source of almost incomprehensible information. "Until the debt is paid. A life for a life. Mine for dad's." The Scythe sang a confirmation. At least he knew that much.

"How do you know when that'll be?" Amanda asked.

He shook his head. "You and dad never knew when a Reaper would knock at your door. I don't know how big they consider your debt. I can ask, but... they gave you a chance at creating life. That seems pretty big to me." He smiled lightly at his father. "But it's worth it. It's worth doing, to keep you with us."

They were quiet for some time. Amanda cried, but promised she was fine. Martin cleared the table when everyone had finished eating, before he and Amanda took Macy out for a walk.

"Do I get the gossip, now?" Jean asked her brother.

"There's nothing to tell," he said. The Scythe sounded off against that statement. "Actually, one thing. I feel weird asking."

"It'll be weirder if you make me guess," she told him.

Jean always knew how to get him to speak. "How do you know if you're in love with someone? Like, really in love with them. There's this girl... I keep thinking about her. I met her yesterday. She's not dead, either, which is a nice change from a lot of the others I've met."

"Do I get a name?"

"Lydia," Ben said sheepishly. "I can't get her out of my head."

"So ask this Lydia out on a date, and see if you really feel the way you think you might. Just, don't start the conversation with the words 'I love you'. That's maybe coming on a bit too strong." He laughed, a sound that felt alien to him after the days he'd had. "Now get yourself to bed," Jean told him. "I'll do the washing up tonight. You can do it tomorrow. Deal?"

"Deal."

He left her in the kitchen, aiming for the squeaky steps on his way up the stairs. Ben had no idea how to ask Lydia out. He'd never been much for the dating scene. Always a wingman, always set up with girls, and never incredibly interested in his friends' choices. A couple of casual girlfriends. One serious relationship in his sophomore year of college. And none of them made him as curious to know more than Lydia May, the undying girl of the Bronx.

Ben landed within his nightmare all over again, swearing to himself as he struggled to find his footing. The sky was well under way of ripping itself to pieces. He remembered it having been faster before, and when he looked around, the people were moving in slow motion, and the debris was barely hovering in place.

A newspaper blew into his hand. His eyes were drawn to one detail, the rest a hazy blur against the apocalyptic backdrop. "January 4th," he whispered. "That… that can't be right."

At the sound of a Scythe screaming in an otherwise silent world, Ben let go of the paper. It zipped out of the sight in an instant. He had no time to worry about it. Before him, the violet Scythe glowed fiercely. The Scythes were ancient and rarely spoke in words he understood, Ben knew. They sang their thoughts to their owners. They were sometimes audible to the outside world. And the violet Scythe was deafening.

It wasn't the volume of the old weapon that bothered Ben, but the sound it was making. If he could equate it to anything human, it would have been pain. Whatever Carlson Grimes was doing to it, it wasn't enjoying the experience.

The body snatcher was smiling, his face burning up under a violet light. Ben could see bones cracking and moving, skin shifting around to accommodate the new shape of the skull beneath. His new body breaking up under the tear in the sky to the song of a pained Scythe, and for the first time since opening the original file of Carlson Grimes, Ben saw his face.

The original body was gone. What Arnold would have called a meat sack had been pummelled until it took a new shape, play dough in the hands of the corrupted Carlson. "Much better," he sneered.

"This is wrong," Ben said to himself. "This isn't real."

He closed his eyes, pinching his leg, trying to get himself to wake up. Within a second, he was soaring through the air. He didn't feel like Carlson had done it. He didn't feel like he'd been thrown. He opened his eyes to see his Scythe swing through the air, stabbing into Carlson's chest, right where he'd burned every victim he'd ever taken.

The violet Scythe quietened down, and light began spilling out of the deformed body. Ben's vision turned red under the power of his own Scythe, and could feel the presence of each soul that been consumed by Carlson during his mad attempt to stay alive for a little bit longer.

Most of the names meant nothing to him, but calling out to him was Lydia May, barely anything left of her. All at once, they were consumed by the red Scythe, from which they would never return.

Ben couldn't scream when he woke up. It certainly felt like he was trying. His throat hurt. His whole body was rigged from the fight. The Scythe was crying in the back of his mind. When he opened his eyes, he squinted against the light coming from his bedside locker, and became aware of the hand pressed over his mouth.

"You were going to wake the whole house," Jean told him. She removed her hand, letting him sit upright. She was sitting on his bed beside him, her eyes full of pity. "They wouldn't tell you, but mom and dad aren't doing too well with this whole thing. They don't want you worrying about them, so they didn't think to mention it, but they need the rest."

"Sorry," he whispered. His voice was hoarse. He didn't want to know how long Jean had been sitting with him.

"Do you want to talk about it?" she asked. "I've seen you have nightmares before, but they weren't like that. You were usually crying." He decided not to argue over that fact; he couldn't remember having nightmares when Jean was around since they were kids.

"It was just a bad dream," he assured her. He didn't believe it, and he doubted Jean would either, but he figured it was a better response than 'You wouldn't understand' or

'It's a Reaper thing.' He was especially afraid that the latter might be true. He had just enough experience of keeping things bottled up inside to deal with the actual Reaping element of his job. He wasn't sure how much he could keep to himself if he continued imagining a confrontation with the body snatcher.

Jean didn't put up a fight over it. "I'm going to try get a couple more hours' sleep. It's almost six, in case you were wondering." She paused by the door. "You can tell me anything. I don't want to have to remind you of that again, okay?" She didn't wait for him to answer, shuffling off to her room next door.

There was nothing to be done from his bedroom. After struggling to eat breakfast, and a quick wash in the sink, Ben was dressed, and pacing back and forth trying to think up a reasonable response to the dream.

"One more day," he muttered.

He had too much on his mind to deal with alone. He waited until seven, and called Gary's phone. He let it ring through on three attempts before giving up. If his supervisor saw his calls, he'd return them.

One more day. The words rang through his head. One more day to see if his dreams were something more. One more day to witness Carlson Grimes rip a hole in the sky. One more day to try stop him, before Lydia lost her soul once and for all.

His heart skipped a beat, and considering how close a look he'd gotten at it after removing his uniform, he wasn't sure that was such a good thing. He needed to know if she was alright, if she was coping okay. Carlson's other bodies had been ruined by his presence.

The Scythe took this as an invitation to take him to her. He landed outside her apartment, almost crashing into the door again. "Seriously?" he hissed. He knocked lightly on the door. The sun hadn't yet fully risen; Ben wasn't sure why Lydia would be awake.

Nonetheless, she opened the door. She was fully dressed, this time, and tried her best to smile when she saw him. "Didn't we already do this?" she asked him. He choked on his response. "I'm kidding. I think. It's hard to tell if anything's funny anymore."

"You're not dead," Ben blurted out.

She shushed him, and dragged him into the apartment. "That is not a corridor conversation, Grim."

"Ben," he reminded her.

"I don't want my neighbours thinking there's something up with me," she retorted. "Think before you speak, okay?" He nodded so roughly his neck ached. "Now, why would I be dead? Aside from the whole 'Your soul is gone' thing you left me with, yesterday."

He shook his head. "I don't even know where to start," he muttered. "You're not the only one whose soul went missing. We're still piecing this together. I just... I can't figure out why you're alive and the others..."

"The others aren't," she finished. "What happened to them?" His eyes fell away from her. He didn't know what to tell her. "Ben, were they killed by someone?" He shook his head. As far as he knew, no. "Were they in accidents?"

"Lydia, I'm not sure this is the right conversation to be having."

"Accidents, yes or no," she insisted.

"No. Not accidents."

She sat down on the couch, burying her face in her hands for a few moments. "Were they sick?" she asked.

"You mean, like a disease? I don't think so."

"Sit down, Ben," she urged. He joined her, keeping some distance between them, even when every bit of him willed him to sit so close they'd practically be touching. Without looking at him, she stated, "Suicide." She grabbed his hand in hers, keeping her eyes covered with the other. "Process of elimination, if they weren't attacked, diseased or clumsy, right? I mean, maybe something else. But you don't want to talk about it, so…"

Ben nodded, even knowing she wasn't watching. "We still don't know much, but we do have a few clues about what happened. I don't think you'll like it" He sighed. Ben wasn't a fool. He knew she'd keep pressing him for answers until he told her everything. "There was a man. His name was Carlson Grimes, and on December 31st, he was attacked in a night-time mugging. He was supposed to die, and he was positive that it wasn't his time. He stole a Reaper's Scythe, and used it to jump from his dying body to another one, a healthy one. Somehow, he ended up inside you, and whenever he left, he took your soul with him."

"I had some friends over that night," Lydia told him. "All from college. We were bringing in the New Year together, before we all really went separate ways." She shook her head. "I thought my ex was acting a bit weird that night. I thought it was just the beer. But it all started to come back to me when I was cleaning up yesterday."

"Do you think there's a chance he might have been Carlson's first victim?"

Lydia frowned, letting go of his hand to search for her phone. He looked over her shoulder as she flicked through dozens of photographs. She held one up to him. "This was taken that night," she said.

Ben recognised the face, just about. "I'm sorry, Lydia," he muttered. "He died a couple of days ago." She stared blankly at the photo. "Were you close? I mean, still close."

"We were trying to be friends. Very casually trying. We shared a lot of friends, and things just didn't work out between us. I thought… I really thought I'd be more upset over him." She put the phone away, and slipped her hand back into Ben's. He wasn't stupid enough to complain. "You know, I didn't sleep last night. I haven't felt like eating in a couple of days. I think… well, I should probably be scared that whatever this guy did to me, he made me a little less human."

The Scythe moaned in Ben's head, but he was clueless to what it was trying to tell him. "I asked someone to look into this for you," Ben told her. "He's a bit of specialist in death."

"Shouldn't you be?"

He shrugged. "I'm new to this. This guy is… older. A lot older."

"Another Reaper?"

"Not in the slightest," Ben said with a smile. "I could take you to meet him. I'm sure he wouldn't mind getting a better look at you."

He had barely finished his sentence when they were thrust onto a patch of grass. Lydia had landed on top of him, rolling onto the grass as quickly as she could. He couldn't hear her complaints or her questions over the noise of the Scythe ringing in his ear. He looked to the side, and saw Arnold's house across the street.

When he'd helped Lydia to her feet, she slapped him. He would have liked to say that it didn't hurt that badly, but even with the Scythe offering him some protection, that would have been a lie. "What the hell was that?" she shouted.

"That was the Scythe, not asking permission again. It doesn't really understand that much." He pointed to the picket-fenced house. "That's where we need to go."

She stopped him. "I never said I wanted to meet this guy. You didn't even tell me who he is. Or where we are."

"We're near Boston, to see a 160-year-old necromancer called Arnold. I wish I could tell you that that was as weird as it got, but you haven't met him yet." She held his arm tightly, refusing to let him walk. "He's safe," Ben told her.

Lydia shook her head. "Whatever. I'll let you explain to him why we're here so Goddamn early."

Ben didn't get a chance to stop her entering the garden, at which point it was too late to teleport them out of there. He had never been more worried that someone would be right about something.

He didn't get to knock, before Arnold opened the door. His hair was messy, his eyes were red and bleary, and he was growing a full face of stubble. Ben didn't think he'd slept. "Something's wrong, right?" he asked. "That's why you're here." He looked at Lydia and frowned. "You two better come in."

Ben led Lydia into the living room. There were books scattered across every surface, though the shelves were still full. Ben concluded that they'd come from the library. He could feel the power coming from some of them, the weight of their words pouring outwardly.

"I'd offer you a seat in here, but I was a little bit preoccupied since your last visit, kid," Arnold told them. "There's tea on the table. Drink up."

"You were expecting me?" Ben asked him.

"Kid, you've got me into a whole heap of trouble here. Of course I was expecting you." He grabbed a book from the chair and carried it with him into the kitchen, ushering his guests along. "There's a theory that certain things are invisible to us until someone makes us aware of them. Usually it's something like an annoying habit someone has. Not like, showing up at my house early in the morning. More like, nail biting, or a really painful laugh. Faces, too. People notice faces more after they've met someone." He placed a hand roughly on Ben's shoulder, forcing him into a chair. "And you, kid, opened up my eyes to a whole cosmic event that's been unfolding. Do you have any idea what that's like for someone like me?"

"A necromancer?" Ben whimpered.

"A neurotic asshole who just wants to stay alive," Arnold corrected. "Something's happening. Something big. Something connected to your–" He cut himself short. "Is this the girl?" He took Lydia by the hand, placing his fingers on her wrist. "Pulse is still strong. Eyes look responsive, if a little on the annoyed side. Exhale." She looked to Ben, and he nodded. She breathed forcefully, and Arnold sniffed it up. After a moment of deliberation, he added, "No signs of inner decay, but could probably do with a mint."

She yanked her arm back. "I'm not a science project," she told him.

"And I'm not a scientist," Arnold remarked. "Sit." She did as he told her. "Drink," he insisted.

"I don't want to," she replied. He stared at her until she took a sip. "Happy?"

"How does it feel?" he asked.

"If was a little more paranoid, I'd wonder if you were trying to poison me," she retorted. "But it's fine. It's a decent cup of tea."

He rolled his eyes. "Firstly, young lady, it's more than decent. Secondly, fine is good. Fine is very good, in fact. You can still drink. You don't look like you have been. Or eating. We can work on that."

"Work on what?" Ben interrupted.

"On making her a little more human," Arnold replied. Lydia and Ben shared a worried glance. "Look, it's the soul. It makes people who they are. Without it, you get the usual mix of despair, emptiness, and a complete lack of drive. And I mean *complete*."

"That would certainly drive a guy to suicide," Lydia muttered.

Arnold looked to Ben for an explanation. "There's been others. At least five more. Four of them killed themselves. The last one... I think he's with Damage Control. Or, he was. He's a bit hurt from yesterday." He told them about his encounter with Carlson; Arnold took notes as he spoke, frowning at his hand writing. Ben wondered, briefly, if it had changed since he'd taken over Mattie Brown's body. "After the fight, they issued me my uniform, and sent me on my not-so-merry way," he finished.

The necromancer looked over his notes, taking everything Ben had said into account with the rest of his studies. "Lydia, you'll need to stay here for the time being," he told her. "That's not a request. I need to make you don't do anything stupid while I figure out how to make you better." She nodded, even smiled, and Ben wondered if maybe she was already starting to recover something of who she was. Maybe Arnold's tea had some magic to it, after all. "Reaper, a moment in the other room."

Ben followed him through, and he shut the door behind him. "What is it?"

Arnold placed a hand on Ben's chest without speaking. "Your uniform. You need to be more careful when you take it off from now on." He didn't give Ben a chance to ask any questions. "I was watching you in there. Are you in love with that girl?"

"In love with her?" Ben hissed. Arnold kept a stern face trained on him. "Okay, maybe a little. But where's the harm in that?"

"There's a lot of harm in it, kid. Never mind the fact that you probably shouldn't be looking to date someone whose soul you were supposed to Reap, whatever your bosses would have to say about that, it's not healthy. It's not…"

"Real?" Ben snapped.

Arnold shook his head. "It's more complicated than that. She might never fall in love again. Do you understand that? And you, well… you were always the sensitive kid, right? And you just yanked your uniform off, and let every human sensation you could possible experience rush back in all at once. Don't lie to me, kid. I've been doing studying Reapers for years."

"You're right. But so what?"

"The uniform is supposed to protect you. The Scythe can't touch you while you wear it. Your bosses can stop you doing something stupid. And it makes your job less emotionally draining. You take that protection away without letting it ease off, and it's like turning everything up to eleven. A little bit of grief can turn into a full-on depressive episode. A broken heart can kill you. And a crush on a beautiful girl with a bit of attitude in need of some rescuing? Kid, what you feel for her is real, but it's not right. Love like that comes over time."

"Why are you telling me this?" Ben asked.

"Because if I'm going to help you, I don't want you doing something that gets us all killed. Forget about the girl, at least until *one* of us does their job right. And kid, Ben, wipe away your tears before she sees them."

Arnold left Ben in the living room, surrounded by ancient tomes and roughly drawn notes, completely baffled at the waterworks he'd put on display. He placed a hand on his chest, right where Arnold had, wishing that his heart would calm down. He sat in the only empty spot in the room, where Arnold had taken his book from. Everything span around him, throwing him off-kilter.

Maybe Arnold was right. Maybe how he felt for Lydia wasn't natural. But it didn't matter. Not while he still felt that way. Not while he could still feel anything for her.

Chapter Eleven: A Dream Made Reality

Ben had not been made aware of any opportunities for days off, but that had been January 3rd: a long, stressful day without a single file interrupting him, without anything taking him away from the necromancer's house, or from Lydia May. Arnold had made some progress with her, convincing her to eat, getting her to display her emotions upon her face even when she was only half-sure she was feeling them, and showing her best to check for injury, just in case her body decided to shut off her nerve-endings at some point.

Arnold tests, his prodding, and his constant warning glances to Ben had worn the Reaper down. When he returned home after sunset, he didn't have the energy to argue about another home cooked meal. Jean kept the conversation simple, Amanda kept her questions general, and Martin tried not to thank Ben any more than necessary. On top of the day he'd had, it was still almost too much.

He thought that he might sleep in for once. He was wrong.

The boom of thunder disturbed from his slumber at seven. He rolled out of bed. It was a marked improvement on the year to date. His sleep had been dreamless, almost tranquil. When the Scythe screamed in his head, he recalled the old expression about the calm before the storm.

"What is it?" he groaned.

Beyond.

The Scythe had never communicated a word so succinctly and clearly to him. He pulled up his bedroom blinds, looking at the sky overhead. It was still dark out, but with the help of the Scythe, he could see the trouble that it had sensed. A miniscule tear, but enough.

"It's started," he whispered.

His phone wailed from his locker, and he answered before anyone else in the house could be woken up. "Ben, we have an issue," Suzie yelled down the line. "Have you looked up, this morning?"

"I saw it," he told her. "I know what this is."

"Well that's a relief, because we're practically clueless," she remarked. "Tell me, Ben, does this have anything to do with your open case?" He thought through his files. Only one was open, as far as Headquarter was concerned. Carlson Grimes. "We recovered two more bodies after your brawl in the streets, a couple of days ago, and four more yesterday. They'd each sustained heavy damage to their bones."

"Which bones, Suzie?" Ben asked, struggling to get dressed while he held the phone to his ear.

"All of them," she stated flatly. "We think we have a location on him, but your file should be more accurate. How big an issue are we looking at?"

He let out a deep breath and slipped his shoes on. He was ready. "I think this might be the end of the world, Suzie, unless we can stop it. And I'm only ninety percent sure I know how."

"I'll match your ninety, and get everyone in on this. But Ben, you have to understand something: Damage Control only has so much jurisdiction here. If you can't stop this, they call in the big guns. The ones they don't write about, anymore. I'm talking Old Testament, stuff."

Kerubiel. Ben shuddered at the thought of what an angel would do to Carlson. "I'll do my best, Suzie. And, stay safe out there, okay? Things are about to get bad."

"Roger that, Reaper," she replied, and hung up. He wished he was wrong, but the storm was only getting started. He didn't need to look to know that when the sound of thunder pounded the house again, the tear in the sky had grown longer.

He willed the Scythe into his hand, just as Jean burst into his room. "What's going on? Where are you going?"

"I don't have time to explain. Just… tell mom and dad I love them. All of you."

"You love… Ben, wait!"

She was too late to stop him. The Scythe pulled him out of the house. They were only a few blocks away, but he needed to check the black file that detailed Carlson's case, and that of the missing Reaper. It popped into his hand out of nowhere, and he scanned through it. The words were swimming all over the page, struggling to remain settled. Ben could only imagine what was happening in HQ, what Rena might be doing to keep up with the impending apocalypse. He thought about the world map of Flight Risks; if this really was the end, all their numbers would be up at the same time.

The Scythe brought him to an intersection, exactly the one he had dreamed of. Carlson stood in plain view in front of him. The rising sun did just enough to illuminate the scene, people rushing out of their houses to see what was happening. Violet light burned around the body snatcher in the distance. Ben could hear him, laughing through two voices. It was more than laughter, though. Ben could make out the sounds of bones snapping. He remembered his dream, and thought now he understood the extra bodies that Suzie had found. Not suicide attempts. They didn't even get a chance.

Carlson had been trying to reshape them in his image, and had failed. He had left half a dozen people to die, before moving on to his next attempt. He wondered if that was all this had been. One big hunt for the right body. Or, maybe, he couldn't keep them long enough to try it. He tried to piece it all together from what Arnold had told him about souls, but he figured that by now he was too late.

There was no point trying to figure out what Carlson was doing. He just needed to stop him.

The other Reapers joined him in the streets. They were silent, deathly figures, each one in uniform. Their Scythes were out, each one a different colour, exactly as Ben remembered it. He hadn't realised how different their robes were, when he had first seen them, slight touches of their home countries weaved into the black.

"We have to stop him," Ben urged.

The closest one looked at him blankly. "You aren't in uniform? Do you realise what that Scythe will do to you if he touches you?" Ben nodded. "Well, you're a braver man than the rest of us, but don't come running to us if this gets out of hand. HQ won't let us act on this until they can figure out what's going on."

"You're kidding."

"I wish I was. We're sitting ducks until someone makes a decision."

Ben looked back to Carlson. Even from a distance he could see the body snatcher's features forming on the new body, the helpless victim whose identity would likely be lost to the world unless HQ had a record of him.

The sky tore open a bit more, and Ben began to hear the screams. It was enough to get the crowd going. Windows began to smash all over the street, people shouted at each other, children cried, and the pieces of Ben's dream began to slot into place. Buildings were torn to pieces under the gaze of Beyond and its billions of souls burning towards the Earth.

"This shouldn't be happening," Ben whispered to himself. The Scythe sang back in response. "It's up to us now, you understand that? I know I'm new to this. I know

I'm not Gary, or any of the others who've served with you. I know I'm not in uniform, and I didn't ask for this job, but I'm all you've got, and we're the only ones who can do anything about this. It's us, or everyone dies, and there's nothing you can do to save them."

The Scythe chirped back at him, and he hoped that they might stand a chance. All he needed to do was get close enough to Reap Carlson's soul. Carlson's, and the dozen others whose souls he'd taken. Ben couldn't understand the choices, especially not Lydia. What made her so special to Carlson that he chose her?

He teleported closer to the body snatcher. His face was red and sweaty, his eyes glowing violet with the Scythe, but he had finished his transformation. The violet Scythe was screaming against the misuse of its power. Ben could feel his own fighting against the noise. He didn't know how to relate the weapons to one another, but for the second time in only a few days, these two were being pitted against one another.

Step one in any case for a Reaper is to enter the scene, Scythe in hand. The summoning of courage aside, that was the easy part.

Step two: locate the person who was dying. That should have been obvious. In the Underwood case, it had been the decrepit old lady. In the Summers case, the young woman dying from cancer. But Lydia May wasn't dying, and Carlson Underwood had so far evaded the Reapers twice. Death was becoming a much more subjective experience.

Step three: convince the dying person to pass quietly. The thundering boom overhead and the choir solo from the violet Scythe were enough to dishearten Ben almost completely. There was nothing quiet about this. He looked to Carlson, whose grin completely took over his face.

"There's something wrong with you," Ben told him. "This is going to kill you."

"Liar," Carlson shouted. The ground shook under Ben's feet. "I am beyond death, now. I shape my body as I see fit. This one won't fail. Not like the others."

"Not like Lydia?"

Carlson laughed. "An experiment. Every teenage boy wonders what it'll be like. Maybe I was curious. Maybe I wanted to know how it felt to walk in a woman's shoes for once. I should have chosen one who was a little less abrasive."

"She was innocent in this. They all were. You've either ruined their lives, or ended them. Don't you understand that?"

The body snatcher's eyes flashed with light, and he licked his lips hungrily. "I understand it perfectly. It was necessary. I refuse to die. I won't let it happen." His expression drooped to neutrality for a split second, but in that time, the Scythe allowed Ben to see through the façade. Trapped within the mess of reformed bone and mashed up muscle, bloodied clothes and a murky darkness that acted as a cloak, Ben could see the souls of Carlson's victims, withered and drained of everything that made them human. The body snatcher was in the midst of it all, nothing pure remaining of him. Whomever Ben was speaking to, he was more broken and fractured a human than Martha Underwood had been.

And, Ben dismally reminded himself, he was armed with a Scythe.

"I have to stop you," Ben informed him. "It's not just my job. You'll hurt the people I care about, and the people who've been helping me with all of this."

Carlson grinned. "Stop me? I'd like to see you try." The violet Scythe swung in a wide arc, shooting out a blade of light that screamed through the air as it approached Ben.

He barely teleported to safety when Carlson had launched another attack. Ben had to trust in his own Scythe to pull him out of danger every time, but it was all they could to keep their distance from the deathly blades of light. They cut through lampposts easily, and sliced up the road like it was soft butter. Ben watched in horror as a blade struck the other Reapers, but they stood their ground, unharmed.

At least, Ben thought to himself in relief, they were safe. There was no telling when they might be needed to step in.

The Scythe blasted images into his head, scenes from around the world where similar tears in the sky were breaking open. So far, the worst of it was contained to the battlefield at the intersection.

In an attempt to dodge another attack from Carlson, who was beginning to utilise the abilities granted him as a corrupted soul – throwing large chunks of broken building with a simple swipe of his hand – Ben ended up in an updraft, gravity pulling him towards the growing tear in the sky.

"We can use this," Ben told his Scythe. He willed the red light into his eyes, and his hopes were answered: whatever was causing the disruptions to gravity, whatever was breaking up the world around him, Ben could see it. The pushes and pulls, the rising and falling, he could see it as rivers flowing in one direction or another. The Scythe sang back a quick response, and he felt himself thrown through the air – up and down as it saw fit to enter different streams, feet never touching the ground.

Carlson was doing everything he could to hit the Reaper, but the sudden swiftness at which Ben was moving was rendering his Scythe's blasts useless. It was a blessing for the young Reaper, who was doing everything he could to keep his stomach settled. He was glad to have skipped breakfast.

A violet blade of light became severed upon contact with the red Scythe when Ben rematerialized in its path. A blink of an eye later, he was in front of Carlson, Scythe's hitting against one another in a flurry of movement that Ben couldn't keep up with. He could hear the Scythes singing to one another, the red weapon issuing forth commands to Ben quicker than he could understand them.

The body snatcher took note of Ben's hesitation in combat, and threw him backwards with a thrust of his hand. The red Scythe had other things in mind. Ben vanished and reappeared behind Carlson in an instant, shoving him clumsily to the ground.

Now.

He thought of Lydia, and how, unless Arnold was successful, this would be the end of her. Maybe the necromancer was right. Maybe he did love her.

But he also loved Jean. And Amanda, and Martin, and Macy. Love wasn't a weakness. It was a cause. It was why he was fighting Carlson Grimes, instead of having his father's funeral interrupted by an apocalypse.

If he didn't do this, either everything he had ever done, from the boring life he'd led to the souls he'd saved, would be for nothing, or the world would see that there were scarier things than a man who didn't want to die. Ben's curiosity about the angel Kerubiel was nothing compared to his fear of the damage an angel's smiting could do.

He pressed the tip of the Scythe against Carlson's chest, to an explosion of light. A long, black thread of light oozed from the body snatcher, red and blue strands weaving through it. Ben could pick out the cries from each one, songs more devastating and incomprehensible than his Scythe's on a bad day. He watched, helpless as Lydia May's mostly broken soul was absorbed into the blade, along with whatever Carlson's soul had become in the process of creating an apocalypse.

The body snatcher began wheezing for air, his skin turning purple. Ben knew he didn't have long, now.

"That was step four. It's over," he told the man.

"I know," Carlson whispered. "Thank you. Thank you…"

Ben edged away from the quickly decomposing body. The violet Scythe disappeared in a flash of light – back to its original owner, Ben hoped. He looked up: the souls were still burning, still falling, the tear still spreading towards the horizon on either side.

"Too late," Ben muttered. "I was too late."

Three days, three battles lasting barely a few minutes, one case of falling in love, not enough sleep and barely enough food caught up with him. Before he could do anything about the damage that was to be done, he collapsed.

In the world beyond the one most people see, there are Reapers. A Reaper's duty is to protect the souls of those who would otherwise become corrupted in an attempt to remain on Earth after their death, and in rare circumstances to ensure the natural order of life and death was maintained. There were seven Reapers, always, working between seconds on every continent, on every small island, hot, cold, drowned or in drought. In their history, as long as humanity has been aware of death, the Reapers have kept a balance in the world, sharing their duty equally.

When Ben Cooper opened his eyes to a bright, blue sky, and a crowd in the hundreds, he began to understand that his job had just become more complicated. He wasn't sure where he was, except that there were more people present than there had been before he had arrived, and that some of the residents were going to have a hard time explaining the morning to themselves.

"Ben," a voice called. Ramirez cleared his way through the crowd to help him as he sat upright. "How're you doing? We'll have a doctor over to you soon. Is your head okay?"

"I think so," Ben mumbled. "What happened?"

Ramirez broke everything down for him as simply as he could. Carlson Grimes was officially dead, soul collection confirmed. The missing Reaper was found in an alley, still in his uniform, having been trapped between moments. Ramirez had been foggy on the details; as he put it, the Reapers had their own way of explaining things, once they'd been in the job long enough, and only half of it made enough sense for regular people to understand. With their collective power, the other six Reapers closed the tear between the Earth and Beyond. It happened quicker than the eye could follow.

"Where are they now?" Ben asked.

"Scattered to the wind. The world saw something today that it was never meant to see, and a lot of people found themselves in jeopardy over it. The soul count is still unconfirmed, but it could have been higher."

Ben looked over the officer's shoulder. Body bags. At least a dozen, by his count. He hoped that was the worst of it, that the tear hadn't done more damage in more populated areas. The town was a wreck, but things had to have been worse here, the source of everything broken and fragile.

"Everyone was worried about the young Reaper who saved the day," Ramirez added. "Detective Bonham wanted me to send her regards once you'd woken up. She wanted to come talk to you herself, but she's busy coordinating efforts around the town. There are a lot of people to explain this to. Somehow, I don't think 'gas leak' is going to work this time."

Ramirez was called away shortly after that, to help recover an old lady who'd gotten herself trapped in the grocery store during the rioting. When he returned, Ben was gone.

Chapter Twelve: A Different Type of Magic

So often where death was concerned, debt was around the corner. Ben Cooper thought that he understood that, between his father's willing sacrifice, his sudden newfound employment, his work in the field, and his meeting with a certain necromancer. It was the latter that most confused him, when he awoke on the couch of Arnold Schultz, a white aura wrapped around him, pouring from Arnold's outstretched hands.

"You really did a number on yourself, kid," Arnold told him. Ben looked down at his clothes. He was covered in blood and cuts. He couldn't remember being hit. "When a Reaper does his work, it's minutes for him and seconds for everyone else. Everything goes so quickly, they barely take notice of minor inconveniences. Most of them are safe in their uniforms, anyway, or protected by their Scythes. Yours worked overtime, I guess."

"How did I get here?" Ben asked.

"I went and picked you up," Arnold explained. "Soon as I heard you weren't dead, that is. I couldn't be seen dragging the corpse of a Reaper away from a battle scene like that. I've got a reputation as it is, without anyone pinning this face to a board and realising who I am."

Ben thought about the board in HQ. If Arnold's face wasn't already removed, it wouldn't be correct anymore.

"You should be fully healed in a few minutes. Just let me do my work."

"I didn't realise you could do this," Ben admitted.

Arnold smirked. "Most necromancers know more than one type of magic. A lot of them specialise in something a little more offensive. I have friends for that. I'm more of a trick-of-the-eye kind of guy, with some old-fashioned healing magic thrown into the mix for variety. Not every person is better off dead to me."

He hushed any further questions, and Ben was left with nothing to do but focus on the sensation of his skin stitching itself back together. His stared at the blood on his clothes, and began to wonder how superficial his wounds had been. Ramirez hadn't seemed too worried about him. No one had. Their focus had been the civilians.

And Ben's was pulled away from his injuries. "What happened with Lydia?" he asked.

Arnold smiled, and the white light faded away. He helped Ben to his feet. The necromancer had black rings around his eyes, and the colour had been drained from his face. He still managed to look at least a bit pleased with himself. "Alive and well, all things considered," he reported. "Would you believe she's actually sleeping? I gave her use of my bed. Don't get jealous."

"Will she be alright?"

The necromancer laughed. "Better than your bosses will be, that's for sure. I heard they didn't let the other Reapers fight. They just left you to deal with the whole mess by yourself, even knowing you'd die if you failed. And only on your third working day?" He led Ben into the kitchen; it seemed to be his favourite room in the impossible house. He set his kettle to boil, sitting his charge down at the table. "The only way to keep Lydia safe from the world was to do to her what I did to myself. Her body is going to be kept in a sort of…stasis. She won't age. Her body remembers who she is, thankfully, so it hasn't completely given up on the idea of living, yet."

"But she'll never lead a normal life," Ben pondered. "Carlson took that from her."

"She was dead the moment he took over her body. But that's my speciality." He got up to make the tea, but his legs gave out on him. Ben took over, guessing from observation how the older man preferred it. "You two... you have me drained. But hey, I haven't felt this young in a long time. It's been too long since I was part of a world-saving team."

"A team?" Ben chuckled.

"Sometimes I can stand to be around other people long enough to work with them," Arnold admitted. "I'm not always very good at it. Most of them want to kill me by the time we're done. They were good times, I tell you."

"Is that why you saved me?"

Arnold frowned. "I don't know. I think maybe I wanted to do something nice for you. Well, something else nice. Keeping you alive is just secondary." That caught Ben's attention, to the point of almost knocking a cup from the counter. "I told the girl that I wasn't a scientist, but I still read. Humanity has come a long way since I was a young man. I found a way to give her some sensation back where she needed it most."

"You're disgusting," Ben retorted.

"The heart, kid. I meant the heart." He let out a burst of laughter, cut short when he clamped his hands over his mouth. "Don't want to have to explain that to Sleeping Beauty up there." He took a cup from Ben, taste testing it. He seemed at least marginally satisfied. "You'll need to give her some time, but there's a good chance that I gifted young Lydia upstairs with the power to feel real, lasting human emotion again."

Ben looked at him sceptically. "How is that a favour to me?"

Arnold winked. "Because I can put in a good word for you, now that she can possibly reciprocate those feelings you accidentally gave yourself for her. You're her dark knight in deathly armour."

They stayed at the table for at least an hour before Ben's phone buzzed with a text message. In that time, Arnold filled Ben in on some of the spells he'd put over Lydia's body, to keep her safe, and about her first rush of feelings when he'd finally figured out how to rewire her body without causing permanent damage.

"She called her mother," Arnold said. "It was really sweet. She said that she loved her, and you know, I think she really meant it. Afterwards she cried a lot, especially when she thought about her ex dying and how she was probably next. That was when I suggested she try sleeping for a while. Do us both a favour." He smirked to himself at that. "Anyway, kid, you should see what they need you for in the Great Nowhere Upstairs."

"I really wish they could have just left me alone for a little bit longer," Ben sighed.

Arnold clapped him on the shoulder. He was looking better, already, and not for the last time did Ben wonder if the necromancer was using a magical blend of teabags. "I'll keep you up to speed on the girl," Arnold promised. "And hey, I think we could work together again sometime. Maybe when we're not looking at an impending apocalypse."

"I might like that," Ben said with a smile.

The moment he stepped through the garden gate, he heard the familiar songs of the Scythe.

"I missed you, too," he told it. He took a long look at the sky. The world was a paint-by-numbers masterpiece, and he couldn't believe how good he felt to live in it. "Hey, before we go to HQ, I have to ask something."

The Scythe whistled back to him. He could only imagine it was trying to make conversation.

"How many Reapers fell in love while they were working with you? How many stood a chance at a real relationship?"

Silence. He hated when the Scythe did that to him. "Maybe it's for the best. I don't think I deserve her, anyway." He looked longingly back at Arnold's house, catching sight of Lydia in the upstairs window. She waved at him slowly, before the Scythe pulled him away.

He would have to work on his exits.

Chapter Thirteen: End

The Reaper Headquarters was very much the way Ben remembered it from his previous visit, except that everyone appeared to be on some sort of drug that caused agitation and anxiety. The administrative staff, which Ben was sure made up ninety-nine percent of the workforce, were doing their rounds, checking through hundreds of files, cross-checking names and locations and attempting to figure out – as best as Ben could tell – whether there was a direct correlation between the tear-points and the increased numbers of people who were suddenly fascinated with the idea of not dying.

The Flight Risks map was quickly becoming a beacon of horror at the thought of overtime. Ben almost laughed at it, except for Rena's glare from behind the desk. "You're not dead," she noted.

"You'd know if I was," he pointed out. He wondered if she'd been secretly looking forward to seeing Kerubiel in action. "I was told to check in."

People began to notice his presence. Their eyes turned to the desk, where Rena and her partner beamed as much as possible without showing true affection for the man in front of them. Ben placed Rena's approval of him as being somewhere above neutral acceptance and somewhere below Kerubiel-levels of fandom.

The room began to applaud, and it took Ben a moment to realise that it was for him. His cheeks burned red under the attention. One person cheered, and the doors to the elevator opened. Upon the arrival of Becky, the room fell quiet again, and the staff resumed their work.

"They aren't used to having a hero in their ranks," Becky told him. "You surprised me today. I'm not used to surprises. Carlson Grimes was also a surprise. We had to figure out what was happening with him, you understand."

He nodded. "You were willing to sacrifice a pawn to save yourself. You still had your trump card to play, if everything went south."

Becky glared at him, then whispered something to Rena. The woman nodded, and made a silent call. Within a few seconds, Gary Murphy appeared in the lobby. Ben barely recognised him behind weary eyes and a face full of stubble. "I heard you did well today," Gary said to Ben.

Ben frowned. "You didn't return my calls. I couldn't get in touch with you before all of this went down." Gary remained stoic. "I thought something had happened to you," Ben muttered. "I needed help, and you weren't there, and I thought something might have happened. Things just kept on happening."

"Mister Murphy had some business to attend to," Becky informed him. "I was made aware of his sudden departure."

"Becky," Gary said warningly. "You didn't call me in for that."

She shook her head. "No, of course not. It's about Ben's contract. You're his supervisor, and his predecessor, so you need to be here for it. This way." She led them to the elevator, and up to her office. It was exactly as Ben remembered, if not greener. The woman seemed to get lost in the foliage, before taking her seat at her desk.

She placed a Bible on the table, and with a simple sigh, silenced the room. The birds no longer sang, the water no longer ran, and the leaves no longer stirred.

"What's so important that you had to bring us here?" Gary asked. "If it was just a contract, you could have just sent him the papers. And why the Bible? That's not procedure."

"Patience," she told him. "Ben, you started here three days ago. In that time, you reaped a total of fifteen souls, when one totals the number of souls collected by Mister Grimes. Ordinarily, that's not great progress, but circumstances do play a role in these things. A missing supervisor, for a start."

Ben looked to Gary, who shook his head. He hadn't thought that his soul-count being so low would actually be an issue.

"At the same time, you also prevented an apocalypse-level event. No Reaper has ever been involved in one, and you managed to succeed without taking an innocent life with your Scythe. Every soul that was consumed by the blade was on the list. It's commendable."

"So commend him, and let us go," Gary insisted.

She nodded, which seemed to take the former Reaper by surprise. "We're here to make you an offer, Ben. To let you decide if you want to leave the job, debts cleared. After what you did, it's the least we can do. You can hand in the Scythe and the uniform, and return to your life." Ben tried to share a look with Gary, to garner some wisdom from him, but his supervisor was staring at Becky.

"And the Bible?"

She tapped the cover of the book gently. "We have reason to suspect that Ben might be special. Incredibly special. The Reapers aren't just personifications of death. They are Death. As Death, you had visions of the end of the world. We think…" Becky shook her head. The hesitation didn't suit her. "We think he may fit into the Christian concept of the end times, as depicted in Revelations. In theory, if he can see the end of the world, it might be a little bit closer than we're ready for. That's both an exciting and terrifying prospect, as I'm sure you can imagine."

"You know how insane this sounds, right?" Gary snapped.

"Take some time to talk it over together," she told them, and stood up from her chair. She left the office in silence, not even her high heels making a sound on the stone floor.

Gary let out a deep breath. "They think you're a Horseman," Gary explained. "As in, one of four, not merely one of seven Reapers. It's not usually a role that comes with a happy ending, if every single apocalyptic scholar is to be believed."

"And what if she's wrong?" Ben asked. He didn't want to think too much about any more impending apocalypses. He wasn't sure he could ever mention them to Arnold. The necromancer might put some distance between them if it ever came up, and that could be the end of any chance he had with Lydia.

His supervisor seemed less concerned with his love life. "Becky's usually right about her speculations, but they don't usually amount to something quite so... Biblical, in proportion. It shouldn't affect your work, anyway, if you wanted to keep it up."

Ben thought about it. He had almost been killed three times, already. That didn't feel like such a big deterrent as he thought it ought to. He had fought, and he had survived.

"The job is dangerous," Gary told him. "Underwood-type cases pop up more commonly than we'd like. There aren't enough Reapers in the world to deal with them, and I don't think it's going to get any easier after today." He looked over his shoulder nervously. "I probably shouldn't say this," he whispered, "but don't expect the praise around here to continue to very long, either. These folks don't know how to keep a smile for more than a few hours at a time." He cracked a half-smile. "But this job, it could help you find yourself. Death has a way of opening one's eyes. It's a fulfilling position, and someone will have to do it, anyway.

I'm pretty sure you can quit any time you like, too, if you find yourself a little bit put out by it all. Worked for me."

The Scythe sang in the back of Ben's mind. He thought it was trying to be encouraging, but sometimes it was hard to tell with instruments of death whether their happiness was a good thing or not. He considered all the times that the Scythe had saved his life. Maybe, he thought, they finally had developed the beginning of a good working relationship.

"I think I can do it for a little while longer," Ben said quietly, afraid that Becky was on the other side of the door listening. "But I'd need proper training, and I need the Scythe to listen to me a bit better."

Gary gave him a gentle smile. "You're going to make a lot of people proud, Ben. And the money's not too bad, here, either," he added with a laugh.

They didn't rush into reporting Ben's decision to Becky. They took advantage of her absence to enjoy the quiet of the room, while everyone else in the building resumed their freak-out at the near-end of the world. Gary was soon to be free of this part of his life, and Ben could happily report home that not only was he a hero, but his parents' debts had been paid off completely. Not bad, he thought, for a few days' work.

Neither of the men knew it, then, but in the space of the few minutes the world had been tearing itself apart, so much had changed. And while the circumstances of Ben Cooper's work as a Reaper had changed, he was charged and ready to do as a Reaper was meant to do: protect the souls of those who cling too deeply to life.

Still, words lingered on his lips that he dared not speak aloud, his eyes resting on the Bible. They echoed about in his head, a space once reserved for whatever nonsense he purported to be at least semi-sensible. If he were a praying man, he might have prayed for the words to leave him altogether, but there they remained, and would remain long after he left the building that afternoon.

"I am become Death, destroyer of worlds."

ACKNOWLEDGEMENTS

I first published this book in 2017, in preparation for my first comic convention in Ireland. Back then, I had a small support team, a handful of other books, and a desire to start putting more work into peoples' hands. I have been fortunate, since the publishing of the first edition of *A Death in the Family*, to make friends and meet readers at events and online that have helped shape me as a person and a writer.

This edition wouldn't be possible without the support of Olivia, Sara, Hedwig, Carrie, and Kat, whose support and encouragement regarding my books – and in most cases, this book in particular – served as motivation to keep working on the series.

A special thank you goes out to my friends at Cupán Fae, with whom I have been lucky enough to work with on a number of anthologies over the last few years. Thanks to Helen, Kat, Tommy, Catherine, Roisin, Sorcha, Yvonne, Quinn, Leyla, Mark, Axel, Eoghan, Ryan, Caitriona, Ellen, and Colm.

Shout-out to Gareth and Gary, my friends from Limit Break Comics who've been rocks to lean on when times were hard, and walls to bounce ideas off when I needed to talk through ideas.

Thank you to Andrew, Ciarán, James, Jessica, Laura, Ciara, Kevin, Karen, and Monica for your friendship and support over the years. I am blessed with long-term friendships.

Finally, thank you to my family for putting up with the constant noise of the kettle as I work on my books.

ABOUT THE AUTHOR

Paul Carroll is a writer and comic creator from Dublin.

His work primarily focuses on the extraordinary, be that through magic, science or just downright chaotic. He is a founding member of both Limit Break Comics and Cupán Fae, Dublin-based creative groups. His obsessions include tea, foxes and spreadsheets.

For free stories, news and updates, visit
paulcarrollwriter.com

Printed in Great Britain
by Amazon